ISBN: 978-1-990217-01-2

Front cover image by Kaitlynn Van Orman
Book design by Stephanie Van Orman
Author photograph by Alison Quist

https://tigrix1.wixsite.com/stephanievanorman
stephanievanorman.blogspot.com
tigrix@gmail.com

If I Tie U Down

A Novel by

Stephanie Van Orman

Other Books by Stephanie Van Orman

Whenever you Want
Kiss of Tragedy
Behind His Mask: The First Spell Book
Hidden Library: The Second Spell Book
A Little Like Scarlett: A Partial Autobiography
His 16th Face

Chapter One
Seven Hundred Dollar Handcuffs

Shannon

"Hey! Are you okay?"

His voice filtered up through my senses. Pain thundered through my skull and rang in my ears so that he sounded like he was calling to me across a distance. He wasn't though. He was right beside me.

Actually, we were handcuffed together.

I stuffed my free hand into my hair. There was blood. Head injuries always looked so much worse than they were. I was probably lying in a pool of blood. Squinting, I looked around. The light was gray and my vision blurred.

"Is there a lot of blood?" I whispered.

"Not really."

"Is there a bad bump?"

"Probably."

I glared at him. "But…"

As my vision cleared I saw his expression was amused, but he had looked pleased by everything that had happened that night. He had a smile on his lips and a chuckle in his throat. It had been infuriating. He even smiled at me over his shoulder when I held a gun to his back.

He grinned like that as he rattled our handcuffs. "Feeling sorry you didn't put up more of a fight?"

"How did you know?" I said, my voice garbled as I coughed.

"I'm Fletch."

He was so loathsome. The whole time he had been insisting that he was Fletch Litman when both Natalie and I knew he was Carver Criche… the biggest loser/liar/weasel I had ever even heard about.

"What did you do to land yourself here, stuck together with me?"

I sighed. "It's not important." I needed to talk as little as possible. "Can you think of a way out of here?"

"No. The last thing I tried," he said, picking up a brick, "didn't go so well for me."

Ironically, it was a brick just like the one that had made the crater in the side of my head. The last thing Natalie said was that she was on her way to the police station to tell them all about the kidnapping. After hitting me over the head, she had obviously handcuffed me to the loser/liar to make sure I didn't bolt. If I actually believed her story about going to the cops, I would have been terrified. If I was a betting woman (and sometimes I was), I bet that Natalie drove to town and got a hamburger at a twenty-four-hour drive-thru. After raising her blood sugar, I believed she'd change her mind about going to the police. Hopefully, she would come back to the campground we had brought the liar/loser to and try to make a deal with the aforementioned weasel/rascal that didn't involve the police.

The way I saw things, even with my banged-in head, the solution was quite simple. I couldn't wait for Natalie to come back. I needed to get the rascal/weasel and me out of the camp kitchen. Breaking the handcuffs shouldn't be too hard, considering where I bought them. Once we were separated, I could conveniently 'lose' him somewhere on the road back to Edmonton.

I looked at the brick he was bouncing in his palm.

In the camp kitchen, there was a stove with a chimney, intended for cooking. It was a million years old, and the weasel/liar had his hand in a hole in the bricks. The other end of the handcuffs was hooked around an even older grill. Natalie and I had done what we could to make sure he couldn't dislodge it. Unlucky for me, I had quarreled with Natalie and now my hand was on the other side of the grill so that I was practically sitting in the fireplace, handcuffed to the most loathsome man. What could I say? I didn't gamble on her being spunky enough to hit me in the head with a brick.

"So, you reefed on your handcuff and brought some of the loose chimney blocks down on you?"

"Yup," he said pleasantly.

I must have missed that when I was outside arguing with Natalie. I didn't know he'd made the slightest attempt to escape. It made me like him better because it made him seem more like a prisoner. This whole time he'd acted so… happy about being with us… like being kidnapped by Natalie and me was his idea of a party.

I was just about to crawl into the fireplace to see if I could get us uncuffed when I noticed the loser/weasel smiling at me again. It was hilarious for him because he knew that I was the girl in the ski mask with the horrible British accent who had ordered him around with a gun. Now the tables had turned and I was also a prisoner. He grinned wickedly at me.

"What?" I groaned.

"I'm sorry if I'm staring," he said, attempting to conceal his amusement. "I just can't figure out why you're here."

"Hmm?"

"Well, when we got here, you two asked me all sorts of questions like why wouldn't I sign the contract and why I was such a douchebag. All questions that make no sense to me because I'm not Carver Criche. You went out. I didn't hear your fight in detail, but then your accomplice attacked you. She dragged you in here, handcuffed you to me and we're done? The chubby one left us here?"

"'The chubby one?'" I repeated. Was that what he thought of Natalie? She wasn't fat. She was just really strong, hence she had been able to knock me out with a brick. I'd never call her chubby. Talk like that was why he was a loser/rascal. "Someone asked you why you were a douchebag and you wondered why?"

He chuckled. "Do you think she's coming back?"

I shrugged noisily.

"Why does that tick you off so much? That I called that woman chubby? She kidnapped me! I could call her a lot worse things, but chubby ticks you off? All things said and done, you have more reason to hate her than me. I didn't make you bleed."

I huffed angrily. "Yeah, well, I might not be very fond of her, but I'm really not fond of a man who only thinks about a woman's sexual appeal."

"And your boyfriend never thought about any of that stuff when he got together with you?"

That did it. I turned myself so my face was out of the fireplace and I could see his horrible, smug expression. "I don't have a boyfriend."

He smiled. "You're more beautiful than your voice under the ski mask hints at, even with the fake accent. Did you know?"

My blush went crazy red. I turned away from him, but he kept talking.

"I'm not Carver. He is the producer for the band, Stark Mad? The band I was playing with tonight is called City of Vines and they were opening for Stark Mad, which is why I was on board their tour bus. I was just saying hi, and when I stepped off the bus, you two grabbed me. You got the wrong guy. I was a replacement drummer. I'm not even a member of City of Vines. When you were out cold, I showed your friend my social media profile and convinced her that although I bear a slight resemblance to Carver Criche, I'm not him. Then I gave her my money clip to handcuff the two of us together and leave. Lovely, isn't it? Sorry that she won't be back."

I swallowed hard. "How much cash did you give her?"

"Seven hundred."

"You had that much on hand? What is wrong with you?"

"It was my pay for the impromptu drumming. They paid me in cash twenty minutes before you picked me up."

I felt like screaming. Natalie owed money everywhere. "You promised her you wouldn't go to the police?"

"Yes, and I won't. Not on her and not on you."

Natalie probably would have done what he asked as long as he promised not to go to the police. The money had been a nice bonus.

"So, Fletch," I said, steaming and feeling like I'd caught an even bigger weasel/creep than I'd originally guessed. "Why do you want to be handcuffed to me in a camp kitchen?"

"This might sound weird," he said, his face out of my view, "but I've heard about you. The famous Shannon Bilx. That's why it's so confusing that you kidnapped me tonight. Why would Simon Crew's ex want to kidnap me?"

"How do you know Simon?" I snapped.

"I'm his cousin."

I refrained from making the tiniest sound. I knew Simon. He was what I would have called a lifer, meaning that he had pursued me off and on for two and a half years. I called all the guys who chased me for over a year, without concrete encouragement from me, lifers. No one ever lasted longer than three years. Simon reached his limit and said goodbye a few months ago, which was fine by me. I didn't keep him around to flatter my ego, even though he did. Regardless of my non-interest, he had been a decent guy.

The thought gave me the sudden, unhappy idea that Fletch was telling the truth about not being Carver and that he might be a good guy if he was close to Simon.

"So, what do you want?" I asked coldly.

"I want to see what Simon found so loveable."

I stuck my head around the corner of the stove and poked my tongue out at him. "Are you finding it?"

A slow satisfied smile spread across his face. He had me exactly where he wanted me.

I continued lashing out. "Or are you going to tell me how awful I am and how no man could ever love me? Don't hold back. I've heard it all before. I'm not even pretty. You should start your tirade by insulting my butt. That's where they always start."

"I didn't spend seven hundred dollars to badmouth you to your face. I'm here to correct you."

I nearly died. "'Correct me?'"

"Yeah. Do you think it's okay to treat people like that? Simon loved you. Why treat his heart like your personal dishrag?"

"Look," I said, preparing to defend myself. "I was not as bad to him as he's let on. Let me tell you the system."

"The system?" he asked with disbelief.

"Yes. The system. You're going to hate me when you hear it, but you might as well get the whole story from my perspective. Everywhere I go, it seems like every guy I meet likes me."

Fletch didn't snort. He looked at me evenly, which helped me like him better.

I continued. "But doesn't that seem arrogant? To naturally assume that every guy who meets me is instantly infatuated? I *am* full of myself, but even so, that seems crazy. Some guys are just flirty. They probably treat every woman they meet like that, right? So no matter what overtures of affection a man might put on for me, I always assume it's nothing until he says something serious."

"Like what?"

"Like, 'I'm in love with you', or 'will you be my girlfriend?'"

"So how do you treat a guy before he says those things?"

"Like nothing. I don't hold hands with him or kiss him on the doorstep, or anything. Usually, I have a collection of guys I classify this way. Everything they do seems to indicate that they like me, but until they say so, I wait."

"Then what happens once he does say something?"

"Usually, I say what I think, which is that I'm not interested. All the time that he's been hanging out, I've been figuring out whether or not I think we'd make a good couple. Almost every time, he isn't what I want."

"So, what happened with Simon, exactly?"

"Exactly?"

"Yeah." Fletch's face was set.

"Same thing. He came around. I thought it was nothing until one night we were watching TV. It was time for him to head home and he started talking."

"Saying what?"

"You know, that I was so beautiful I took his breath away."

"Wait. That sounds like an okay line to me."

"It is," I conceded. "It just would have been better coming from a different man. He was a little different than the other guys though, as in he didn't demand a monogamous relationship with me. If he had, I would have thrown him out the door. He didn't say he loved me. He didn't say he wanted anything. He merely expressed an appreciation for my appearance and that he wished our relationship was something more. I don't deal in that kind of ambiguous crap, so I let him go home without acknowledging a confession of any kind."

"Did you ever kiss him?"

"No."

Fletch looked surprised. "I owe you an apology. All this time, whenever he spoke about you, it sounded like you two were dating, and you were blowing hot and cold. Were you dating him?"

"I went on dates with him, but there was never any kind of commitment. And I resent the accusation that I blow hot and cold. I only blow cold."

"Were you aware that he was deeply in love with you?"

I rolled my eyes. "It may seem snotty to you, but I can hardly keep track of all the guys who are *deeply in love with me*. Sometimes, men, I would barely call acquaintances, have confessed that they love me. I have other things to occupy my mind. I can't be bothered with what a man *might* be thinking when he can't be bothered to open his mouth."

"If I'm understanding you properly, Simon never had a chance with you and all along his feelings have just been a sad, unrequited love?"

I nodded. Then I examined Fletch's ponderous face, hoping our conversation had reached its conclusion. "Does that mean we're done? Look, I'm sorry we picked you up if you were the wrong guy."

"Does that mean you're going to go kidnap the right guy if I let you go?"

"No. That was something I was helping Natalie with, but let's be clear, if there was such a thing as the 'right' guy for me, I'd kidnap him if I wanted to." I winked.

He paused.

I put my head back in the fireplace to see if I could figure out how to unchain us when he suddenly said, "We're not quite finished. You have to tell me exactly what is wrong with Simon."

"Doesn't that seem a bit grueling to you? I mean, would you honestly want to hear every detail as to why a woman didn't want you?"

"Yes."

"You're sick. Simon is a great guy, but his being a great guy isn't a good enough reason for me to date him or fly to the moon with him. It is a matter of compatibility. Unfortunately, loads of men just see something pretty and they think that's the woman for them. They don't know what they want." I grabbed the grate and started yanking on it. "I hate watching sports on TV. The sound of it rankles my nerves and Simon liked to watch football. I hate football the most. I used to kick him out when he would turn it on. I could never live with someone who liked watching sports on TV, and why should he turn me into Lady Macbeth by making him watch his favorite thing on the tiny screen of his phone with his earbuds in? We're incompatible. He should be with someone who enjoys the same things he does."

"Well, what do you enjoy?"

I made a face at him. "I never tell."

He laughed. "You never tell people what you like?"

"No. I never do. If I do, I know men who would turn themselves inside out to be whatever I want. Though I do think that telling Simon to turn off the TV before my ears started bleeding should have been enough of a hint."

"Wait. Are you telling me that you and he hung out for years and he never knew what you like?"

"Of course. Did you know that the word 'romance,' the word 'seduction,' and the word 'mystery' all mean the same thing?

Once someone knows all about you, the romance will be over. Not the love, the romance."

"You're scared to let go of the romance because if someone really knew you, they couldn't possibly love you?"

It was in that second that I realized I had laid myself bare in front of someone I shouldn't have. My theories about dating weren't exactly top secret, but I didn't realize they could be used to dissect me. I had always thought my taste in books, my hobbies, my passions, and my ambitions were the things to keep quiet about. He had seen through me. It was a particularly distasteful experience.

I withdrew from him.

"I'm sorry. You're not wrong… about Simon," Fletch's mellow voice sounded from the other side of the chimney. "If you're not compatible with him then he didn't do anything wrong and neither did you. Also, it sounds like he wasn't very daring in love. If he had been, you would have rejected him and he would have started to heal much sooner. You don't have anything to be ashamed of."

I didn't dare look at him.

"You see, he mentioned you almost every time I saw him. After I heard you'd dumped him, I wanted to get you alone, so I could set you straight. This conversation has been a revelation. I thought you were the kind of girl who dumped guys for kicks. You're just looking for the right man and he hasn't shown up. Am I right?"

"I guess," I mumbled. I got on my knees in the fireplace and started looking at the grate more carefully. It looked like I might be able to get my handcuffs unhooked if I bent one of the bars.

It was pretty tough iron and the nosy man wasn't at an angle where he could help. I messed with it for a few minutes without success when I heard him say something. It was a muffle. "What was that?" I asked, coming out for a break. My hands were sweating.

"Want to try something with me?"

"Are you going to try pulling on the handcuffs instead of letting me do all the work?"

He chuckled. "Why would I do that? They're still doing what I want them to."

"You haven't got what you want out of me yet? What's left?" I exclaimed.

"A date."

"A date? With Simon? I've been on tons of dates with Simon. He's had his chance. Leave me alone."

"You've got the wrong idea," Fletch corrected. "Obviously a date with Simon is ridiculous. I'm talking about a date with me."

I groaned. "Now you've got romantic ideas about me? Forget them. I'm not for you."

"Do you already have someone in mind?"

I shook my hand like I was shaking off the idea. "No. It's just that you're a drummer. I already told you that noise bothers me. The only thing I can think of that would be worse than dating a guy who likes watching football is a drummer. The idea makes the inside of my ears hurt like someone just shoved a needle in each one."

He blinked. "You get more intriguing by the moment. I don't think my drumming should be a barrier between us."

"I do."

"I'm actually a xylophone player with the city orchestra. I was just doing the drumming as a side thing. It was a favor for a friend. Trust me, if you were my girlfriend, you wouldn't be touring sleazy bars and packing drum kits."

I paused and let my breath out slowly. Why hadn't I thought of it before? "You have the keys to the handcuffs, don't you?"

"Yes."

It was an impossible situation.

"Do you have a phone?" I asked, thinking of how my phone was still in Natalie's car. I felt so powerless without it. If I had my phone, I wouldn't have tolerated Fletch's interrogation. I would have called for help immediately. I had a head injury! The first person I would have thought to call would have been Natalie, except now that she thought blunt force trauma was a part of our friendship, I doubted I would ever call her again.

"Yup."

"Good," I said, realizing that 'losing' him on the way back to the city was no longer an option. Instead, I'd have to work with him to get home. "Why don't you hurry up and unlock us while I explain to you why a date with me isn't a good idea."

"I can't wait to hear your reasoning." He chuckled, produced the keys from his pocket, reached up to unlock the handcuffs, and accidentally let them slip from his fingers. I couldn't see where they landed. I only heard the sound of them clattering on the cement floor.

Natalie and I were right the first time. He was the worst.

I didn't say anything while he fumbled around trying to retrieve the keys.

"You know what I think?" I said, after pondering.

"What?"

"I think the only reason you want to date me is to show Simon, and anyone else, that you can. I'm a trophy and you want to win me, just so you can show that you're better than them. You don't know me. I didn't enchant you. You only know me by reputation, and that reputation is what you want to date and not me. You're confused though."

He didn't reply. He was embarrassed about dropping the keys and was still wriggling the toe of his boot to try to pull the keys within reach.

"You're confused…" I continued when he didn't respond, "because you don't recognize that getting together with me would not be winning anything. I'm not actually fun. I'm like a cat that looks adorable in the shelter. You take it home expecting it to give you love and cuddles and it only scratches the hell out of your furniture. You said it, if anyone really knew me, they couldn't love me."

"Your argument is interesting, but it won't make me change my mind," he said triumphantly as he swept the keys up in his palm. "I didn't ask you to marry me. I just want to see you in all your glory. I want to see what you're like when you pour on the charm. Is that too much to ask?"

"Oh!" I exclaimed. "That sounds amazing!"

"It does?" he asked curiously as he successfully unlocked the handcuffs.

"Yes, it does!" I turned to face him. He looked a bit battered. We had just spent the night in a deserted camp kitchen, and he looked less sleek than he did when we kidnapped him, but he had some appeal: a touch of attractiveness at his lips, in his smile.

"Why?"

"Because, I'm always worried about taking things too far, being too charming, looking too good, being all that a man wants so completely that if I leave him, he'll never get over me. I'm always holding back, but if you just want to see what I'm like out on a date, I can be all those things I never get to be… and you'll know. You'll know I'm putting on a show and that will be it. It sounds really fun."

"So you'll go on a date with me?"

"Yes! It's only one date." I got up and looked around. "Although, you do have to get me home first."

"I'll be honest, I don't even know where we are."

"We'll work it out. Is Friday night good for you? It's good for me."

Chapter Two
Little Black Dress

Fletch

I did not expect much as I waited in the atrium of the theater. Shannon said she wanted a date on Friday night. Well, that Friday night was a ballet I would be accompanying as part of the orchestra. I didn't know if Shannon liked ballet. I asked her, but she replied that she didn't tell her dates what she liked.

"You want the *whole* experience, don't you?" she said when I asked her.

I waited in my orchestra togs by the front door. I shouldn't have been there, but I wanted to make sure she made it to her seat before I deserted her for the pit.

Nothing could have prepared me for when she came in the door. I had seen a lot of finely dressed people in theater atriums. They didn't turn my head, but Shannon turned everyone's head collectively.

She wore a black dress that made all other black dresses look like hopeless imitations because the woman in the dress had to be Shannon if it was going to look good. It was almost sleeveless but covered the curve of her shoulder. The neckline hit a sweet spot on her chest. The spot showed she was a fine woman under the dress without making her look cheap. As my eyes traveled downward, I suddenly knew why she said men attacked her butt when they insulted her. It was her hips they were going to miss when she was gone.

Reaching up to take her hand, I noticed she wore three thin bangles on her wrist, the only jewelry she wore. Her hair was styled in voluminous curls that looked soft and touchable. Otherwise, it seemed like she was shining, either from her mood or some glitter she'd artfully brushed herself with.

I welcomed her, handed her a program, and rushed her through the ticket area down to the seat I'd managed to find for her.

"I'll take you out for something to eat afterward," I said as I left her to join the rest of the orchestra.

From the pit, I tried to see what she was doing as the performance commenced. Half the time, her head was bent down over her program. At least *Cinderella* wasn't a downer, I thought as I lifted my triangle. I felt like a bit of a juggler as I moved from instrument to instrument. At one point, I was thwacking a wooden block. It was not a very glamorous job, but at least I wasn't shouting at a referee through a TV screen.

Afterward, I met Shannon in the atrium. I expected to see her looking frazzled and tired. The ballet had been three hours long, but she looked just as radiant as she had when she stepped through the doors.

"I guess you don't hate ballet?" I remarked.

"I don't?" she asked innocently.

"Of course, you don't. If you were willing to throw Simon out for turning on a football game, you'd certainly discard me for making you watch a ballet if you didn't want to."

"I've never been to the ballet before," she said.

"Did you like it?"

She smiled and evaded the question. "I made you a present," she said as she returned the program I had given her.

"You *made* it?" I asked skeptically.

"Yes."

I took it from her and was about to open it when several members of the orchestra suddenly appeared. They waved at us and were about to walk by when one of them realized that Shannon was with me. He turned back, "Fletch, is this your date?"

The guy that had stopped was a world-class violinist. His name was Rodderick, and I disliked him, but suddenly less than usual. He would never have stopped to speak to me if Shannon hadn't been standing next to me. Her claims that she attracted all men seemed valid. Rodderick and I had nothing in common, except perhaps that both of us wanted to be near her.

All at once, I knew exactly why my cousin, Simon, had wanted Shannon and why it had bothered him so much that she had not wanted him back. This was her in her element. The way she greeted my band-mates, tossed her curls, and practically made eyes at them was completely loveable. She even showed she was with me by slipping her arm through mine and rubbing my tricep in a show of intimacy. I didn't know if I'd ever been with a woman who actively promoted me in public.

"How did you two meet?" Rodderick asked her.

She smiled wickedly. "I put a gun to his back and told him if he didn't come with me, I'd shoot him."

I stared. How had she delivered that line so well? She didn't sound crazy, merely playful.

Rodderick looked like he was having a malfunction with the saliva in his mouth. She was mouthwatering. "Was it a real gun?" he finally asked.

"Not the kind that would have hurt anyone. That's why I had to jab it into his back, so he wouldn't recognize it was only a pellet gun."

"Very inventive, but that can't have been your first meeting."

I was about to elaborate when I suddenly realized I was more interested in hearing how Shannon would describe the event.

She turned and gazed at me longingly before turning her attention back to Rodderick. "It was just a little trick to get his attention, and to see what kind of man he was."

"Huh?"

She leaned forward conspiratorially. "I took a bit of a chance. He could have turned around, disarmed me in the blink of an eye, or he could have gotten scared and whiny."

"What did Fletch do?"

She smiled her hundred-watt smile. It was the first time she'd done that in front of me and I felt my heart lurch in my chest. "It was better than either one of those things. He threw a smile at me over his shoulder. That's his reaction to having the barrel of a gun shoved in his back. That's why getting together with a percussionist is the best. They know how to strike a girl just right."

I couldn't believe she had actually said that. It was completely embarrassing, corny, and terrible, but very funny.

I laughed.

It was the first time she heard me do that. Most of the time, I laugh with my eyes or chuckle in my throat, but I don't laugh outright.

At that second, Rodderick figured out why the two of us were together. He backed off a step. "You're just joking about the gun," he said because he realized that kind of joke was our sense of humor as a couple, and he didn't like it because it was a joke meant only for the two of us.

It was funny how she had done that. It was like she had drawn a line that included everyone and then suddenly contracted it, so it only included us.

We said goodbye, wishing everyone a pleasant evening.

When we were out of earshot, she said, "You don't like that man, do you?"

"He's very arrogant," I replied.

She nodded.

I had my overcoat hanging from my free hand the whole time we'd been talking and now I threw it over her shoulders.

"I have a table reserved at a Greek restaurant down the street. It might be cold out. You know, there's a reason why women wear furs to the theater. It gets cold."

She looked at me. "I would never get cold when I'm with you."

I looked back at her. My mouth had filled with saliva the same way Rodderick's had. I swallowed and commented patiently, "That's the sort of comment I would consider to be blowing hot."

"That little thing?" she said, diminishing her compliment. "Walk with your arm around my waist. If we cuddle, I won't feel bad for taking your coat."

We walked. She entertained me with prattle so charming, I was disappointed when we got to the restaurant. Once inside, I was suddenly aware of how the building seemed to be crumbling around us and wished I had sprung for a better place. After all, I was probably never getting another date with Shannon, but she loved it. She walked in and told me how interesting it was. She pointed out spots of decor around the room I had never noticed and praised them.

I helped her ease out of my coat and saw the three bracelets on her wrist. She put her hand to her hip briefly and the metal clacked against itself in a sound that was almost musical.

"I get it," I said, suddenly.

She turned to face me, letting her hand bounce up and then return to her hip. "You get what?"

"I get one of your tricks." I pulled her chair out for her and let her sit down.

"Tricks?"

I sat down across from her. "Yes. Your best feature is your hips. You know that, so instead of wearing a necklace intended to draw attention to your breasts or dangling earrings intended to draw attention to your throat, you wear bracelets to draw the eye down to your perfect, shapely, hips."

She laughed, less guarded than before. "No. You're wrong."

"Am I?" I asked, my eyes level.

"Yes. All my features are my best feature. I do wear necklaces and earrings for exactly the reasons you mentioned, but I also wear belts to accentuate my waist. I wore the bracelets tonight especially for you because I thought they would make little tinkling sounds, almost like a bell, and you would like that."

I stopped and considered how much thought had been put into such a small detail. Again, I didn't know if any of the women I had ever dated had noticed something like that about me or tried to please me. It was a little exciting that she had.

She picked up her menu. "Though I do have to say, even though all my features are my best feature, I don't get as many compliments on my hips as my other parts. Maybe people think it's vulgar to tell a woman she has nice hips or something."

"Before, you said that's how unsuccessful lovers attack you?"

She nodded.

"Well, they can be polite until they're rejected. *I* can be honest. Your beautiful hips are probably causing you more problems in the men department than you realize. They're stunning."

She looked at me, clearly reacting to what I said, but I didn't think she would tell me how she felt. Either she was annoyed or moved. It was hard to say from the expression on her face.

I guessed she was moved, because she suddenly asked me, "Do you mind if I order for both of us?"

"I suppose not," I said. It was my favorite restaurant to eat at after a performance, so I'd eaten everything on the menu.

Shannon waved over a waitress and ordered drinks and five different appetizers for us to share. When the food came, she dipped a torn piece of pita bread in hummus and motioned for me to open my mouth.

"What are you doing?" I asked. "I can feed myself."

"You wanted the whole experience," she reminded me with a light in her eyes.

I chewed. When my mouth was clear, I asked, "Do you always feed your dates?"

"Sometimes I sit on their laps," she replied. "You can eat the wings by yourself."

At the end of the meal, I popped into the bathroom to check my teeth. When I came back, I went to the till to pay, and the server informed me that Shannon had already paid the entire bill. I'd never had a woman pay the whole bill before.

I returned to the table.

"Where's your car?" I asked.

"I don't have one."

"I'll drive you home then," I offered.

She picked up the program I'd left on the table and slipped it into my hand. "Don't forget this. I don't need a ride."

"You'll freeze."

"I live close to here."

"You do? I'm always down here. How come I haven't seen you before?"

"It's a big city, but I really do live just six blocks from here. Want to walk me home?"

I did. I covered her in my coat and we stepped back onto the city streets.

As soon as we were outside, she turned to me and said, "Now the date is over and you may tell me your impressions."

"You're poison," I replied. "Which direction are we walking?"

She pointed, and we started moving.

"Did you feed Simon?"

"Often. Usually just popcorn, but yes."

"Did you pay for his meals?"

"Sometimes. Mostly because he paid for mine sometimes. I just tried to keep it fair. Tonight I paid for yours as a bit of an apology for the inconvenience of last weekend."

I didn't respond to that, but asked, "Did you dress up like this for Simon?"

"This is how I look on a Friday night," she replied.

"Of course, it is. You're charming, but I have to ask you. What is your goal when you go on a date? Is it just to make the man weak in the knees? You want him to think you're spectacular when you're with him and hurting him afterward is just an unfortunate side effect of this whole show you like putting on?"

She smiled. "I put in so much more effort tonight. You got all the good stuff. I told you, I wanted to go on a date where I got to be myself instead of worrying about whether or not I would hurt you. You already know I'm a rat."

"That doesn't make it any easier."

"No?" she gasped in surprise.

"No. I want you so much my insides have turned to liquid and knowing you won't have me is a bit much. I'd leave you here if I didn't want my coat back."

"Fletch," she said with a click of her tongue. My name on her lips felt like she'd broken a bone. "I'm taking you home."

"And what does that mean exactly?" I asked suspiciously.

"I'm showing you where I live."

"So I can become like Simon? Become a man who stops by your place whenever I'm lonely and bored? You feed me popcorn, but place boundaries between us so I can never hope for anything more?"

"What are you saying?" she asked cautiously.

I had been about to say, "That won't do for me. I have to have you all to myself. Be my girlfriend!" I had been about to say that when I suddenly realized that was exactly the wrong thing for me to say. She had told me she rejected men when they requested a monogamous relationship. I had been just about to demand one. If she hadn't told me that little hack to deal with her, I would have done what every other man did when they went on a date with her.

I decided I needed to cool the frick down.

"I live around here too," I feigned. "Closer to the theater, but a loft apartment over an essential oil shop."

"Fragrances by Evelyn? I know where that is!" she replied excitedly.

"I bet you do," I said drolly.

"This is me," she suddenly said. It was a tall brown building with a few shops on the main floor.

We were not quite at the doorstep. Knowing the traditional nature of what happens on a doorstep at the end of a date, I stopped her a few feet from it and turned her to face me. "I'm not going to have a relationship with you like the ones you've had with other men."

"Of course not," she said, matching my level of seriousness.

"I'm not asking you for anything," I reiterated.

She nodded.

Then I kissed her. I put my hands under the coat she was wearing and for a moment, my hands were all over her back, her waist, her neck, and at that beautiful curve that led to her hips. She kissed me back. Obviously, being the ice queen had not left her very satisfied, but it wasn't my job to satisfy her that night. In one glorious motion, I stripped the coat from her and the kiss ended.

She shivered, her arms hugging herself instantly.

I took a step away from her. "Good night, Shannon."

She stuttered a goodbye to me as she stepped onto her doorstep, chilly from the sudden removal of my coat, my body heat, and my presence. It would do her good to finish a night feeling a little chilly. After all, that was what she had done to so many men.

I slid my coat on and strode away from her with a bounce in my step I hadn't felt in years.

Back at my apartment, I finally pulled out the program she had returned to me and flipped it open. She'd mangled it. At first glance, her pen strokes looked like juvenile defacing. As I examined the marks more carefully, I realized they looked bad, not because what she wrote wasn't interesting, but because the pen did not want to write on paper that glossy and she had not had a hard surface to write on.

In the margins, she wrote about how the music made her feel, with particular mention of how the music *I* played made her feel. Like the whole orchestra was nothing without the briefest tinkle I made with my triangle. It was the sound of a baby star being born.

Okay, that had been cute.

On another page, she described me and how infuriating she found me when we first met. It wasn't exactly complimentary. It wouldn't have been complimentary from another woman, but from her, the whole thing had a different flavor. Simon would have given his left arm to get under her skin so thoroughly.

On the second to last page, she wrote her address in the margin and said that if I ever decided to throw away the program she'd written me, she wanted me to mail it back to her. She'd pay for the postage.

On the very last page, she had written, "Kiss me at the end of the night."

I felt vindicated.

Chapter Three
The Way He Texts Me

Shannon

As I approached my apartment door, I saw an open dirty diaper on the floor. I knew instantly that it wasn't a real dirty diaper. It was a chocolate bar melted inside a diaper. That was how Natalie's sense of humor worked. I bent down, scooped it up, folded it in half, and opened my door. There was a note that had been pushed under the door with some effort. It was crinkled because it had been almost impossible to get something as thick as a piece of paper under the door.

It said, "Sorry about last week. Your phone is in the diaper."

I tore the lining out and yes, my phone was there. It was dead. I plugged it in and pulled my high heels off. I'd just walked six blocks in them.

Fletch had been a good date. I tried to figure out why. Immediately, part of the appeal was clear. He'd been on the other side of the theater the whole night. That prevented him from making the same sorts of mistakes other men made. For example, he did not talk to me when I was trying to pay attention or make so much noise that he bothered the other people in the theater. At no point in the date had he tried to sneak his hand up my thigh or snake his arm around my waist without my permission.

In the end, it boiled down to one thing. He had spent the evening as my date but concentrated on something important that was not me. I liked that. I got bored with a man showering me with attention for hours on end.

The date with Fletch had been perfect. I arrived, made the proper impression on him, he'd left to play with the orchestra, we went to dinner, and he walked me home. He had his hands on me the appropriate amount of time for a first date. He hadn't said anything stupid while at the same time making it very clear that he was attracted to me.

I sat on a blush velvet pouf and rubbed my feet through my stockings. I didn't know what to do. Normally, I would not call a man and invite him on a second date. Normally, I would wait for him to ask me out. If I called Fletch, what would that mean? That I wanted to date him? How much power would that give him?

Then I realized something I did not like. I never wanted to go on dates with the men who took me out. They always had high expectations of what a woman like me could give them. I didn't like the pressure. When I had been with Fletch, there had been no pressure. He expected nothing beyond the one date. Perhaps that was the core of his appeal.

I got up and went into the kitchen to think about that.

By then, my phone was charged enough that I could restart it as long as I kept it plugged in. There were roughly forty text messages. A few of them were from Natalie and they had been sent in the last two hours.

I dealt with her first, typing out, "Just forget the whole thing."

I had to put a lid on that situation one way or another because I still had to see her. I worked for a recording studio, not as a sound tech, but as an administrator. Natalie was a singer with pipes like Adele and she couldn't get a break. Carver Criche had treated her very badly, always promising to help her with his vast web of connections and never coming through. He was a bit of a legend in the industry, not for jerking artists around, but for getting results. If he helped her, she'd get the break she needed.

For me, the problem was that I loved trouble. I loved getting into trouble. I loved hijinx and pranks and being somewhere you shouldn't be in order to have something outrageous happen. That was how I'd gotten looped into prodding a young man in the ribs with a fake gun. It was dumb… and kind of awesome. I never would have pulled a stunt like that by myself. I wasn't the right build to force anyone to do anything. If I had been alone, any man I pulled a gun on would have me on the ground in less than a minute. Natalie's muscle had made kidnapping Fletch possible.

Except obviously, it wasn't supposed to be Fletch. It was supposed to be Carver.

Ever since she knocked me out with a brick, I began to wonder if Carver knew a thing or two about Natalie that I didn't know. Maybe there was a reason why she wasn't a superstar that I hadn't been able to see. Whatever. It didn't matter. I'd been fooled into thinking she was a victim and maybe, despite everything, she still was… I just couldn't help her anymore.

The second most recent text was from Simon. He was asking me if I was on a date with his cousin with furious undertones.

I pulled up the message. "Yes, I was out with Fletch tonight. At the ballet."

"I bet you just loved that," he replied with an emoji of a football tacked on.

I didn't reply and continued down the list of people who had texted me: my sister, my other sister, my other sister, my sister from another mister, my mom, my sister's MIL (who wanted to borrow my wheat grinder), and Fletch.

I sat up. It came in with a new batch of messages my phone had retrieved and I didn't notice it when I was busy typing to my family that I wasn't dead, I had just left my phone somewhere.

Fletcher's text was direct. "Do you want to see me again?"

"Aren't I poison?" I replied.

"Yes or no?" was the next message that popped up on my screen.

He was good. I could have sent him misleading, yet flirty, text messages for a month without answering.

I looked at the screen and smiled. I liked directness.

"Yes," I typed.

"When?" he wrote back.

I didn't know the answer to that. I'd been without my phone for a week. I knew my sisters wanted me to go shopping with them the next day, and I didn't know when we would be finished.

Sunday?

"Library date on Sunday?"

"I'll meet you at two." Then he typed, "Good night, adorable rat."

And even though I typed various things to him to try to get him to have a conversation with me, he didn't type another thing. He was out for the count.

Chapter Four
Vandalism for Beginners

Shannon

I sat down at a table on the second floor of the library and waited for Fletch. I was early because I wanted to watch him enter the library the way he had watched me enter the theater on our last date.

He walked through the doors and I studied him as he strode around the main floor, looking for me. I could have texted him at any time to let him know where I was, but I didn't. I wanted to watch him walk around.

It was no wonder that Natalie and I thought he was a big-time music producer. His whole aura said that he was someone to take notice of. His hair was auburn and cut short in the back and left long on the top in a way that was a little less than cutting edge style. Like he didn't need to follow trends. He could do whatever he wanted.

His most noticeable feature was his mouth. In particular, his teeth. That was why his smile had been so notable the first time I'd met him. His teeth were white, strong, and very rectangular. When he spoke, flicking his tongue against those perfect teeth, his words seemed crisp, tantalizing, and almost like the words themselves took on a life of their own. It wasn't just memorable, it was mesmerizing.

Above that smile, he had gray eyes with red winglike eyebrows that gave the impression that he was part mythical creature. I decided he looked as if he were half humans and half phoenix as he spotted me and got aboard the escalator.

He approached the table, and said casually, "A library date? I was anticipating an empty alley. Maybe you'd have a backpack with a few cans of spray paint."

"What makes you think I would do such a thing?" I asked, sounding scandalized. The truth was, I vandalized stuff all the time. That was actually what our date in the library was supposed to be about, introducing him slowly to my world. I had planned to work my way up to talking about graffiti. How did he know already?

As he sat down across from me, he had that ridiculous smile plastered across his face again. I felt the drawstrings on the layers of my reserve grow slack when I should have been mad that he knew my secret.

"What are we doing here?" he asked casually. "Are we going to look for my favorite book?"

"We certainly wouldn't be here to look for *my* favorite book," I joked paradoxically. "Look at this." I pushed a hardback toward him.

He looked at it the way a person who reads looks at a book. He looked at the cover, taking a moment to absorb the art, then turned it over and read the back.

"Does it look interesting to you?" I asked, licking the center of my top lip in anticipation.

"It's a book about a girl who fell down a well," he said levelly.

I shook my head playfully. "You are not looking at it correctly. What the book is about is a side note in this story." I opened the back of the book to those precious blank pages at the end. Inside the book, was a letter. I showed him the handwritten words.

"Oh?" he said, reaching forward and taking the book from me. He read the letter silently, his eyes dashing across the page. When he was finished, he looked up at me. "That was pure beauty. Did you write this?"

I shook my head. "I found that book here one afternoon when I was very bored. Have you ever been bored?"

"Of course."

"No, I mean, have you ever been bored for years? Like lethargy is the essence of your soul? Like movement is a lie because it will never get you anywhere? You're dying a slow death and when you do die, nothing that was once a part of you will remain?"

Fletch looked at me cautiously.

"One day," I continued, "while feeling this way, I was in this library and I found that letter written at the end of that book. It changed me. I decided I didn't want the marker of my life to be on a tombstone in a cemetery no one ever visited. Instead, I wanted marks of my existence to be everywhere… on everything."

"Really?" he said longingly, pondering my face. "What do you write?"

"Something I want everyone to read. Sometimes I draw. My art isn't as good as my writing. Sometimes I spray paint. What gave me away? You asked me if I had spray paint in my bag when you got here."

"You have paint on the bottoms of your shoes. It looked like spray paint. I saw it because you had your feet propped up on a chair as I came up."

I put my foot on my knee and examined the paint stains. "I can see I'm going to need to be more careful."

He leaned forward. "Why are you telling me this? I thought you never told your dates about yourself?"

"I don't usually. I wonder why I'm doing this…" I said, lifting my eyes to look across at him with my most beguiling expression.

He hesitated before he spoke. The hesitation pleased me. "I think I know why."

"You do?"

"Yeah. Most people probably wouldn't understand you defacing the inside of a bus or an electrical box. Have you had bad experiences confessing to it? Suddenly a man isn't so charmed by your beauty because he can only think about how defacing public property is probably a symptom of mental illness."

I was appalled, but I refrained from reacting. Slowly, I said, "Have I answered all your questions about me then? Do you understand now why men like me and why they can't have me?"

"You have not answered a tenth of my questions," he replied, peering at me from under his red eyebrows. Even though he had said that line about mental illness, it was clear he did not share that feeling. "Were you planning on writing in these books?" he asked, indicating the pile of books next to me.

"I was only going to place post-it notes."

"Cool. Show me."

I took a book off the top of the stack. It was a romance novel that looked to be on the erotic side. My post-its were the shape of faceless pink teddy bears. I got out a sharpie and wrote on the top note, "Do you like being licked?" I tore it off and put it in the middle of the book, without any edges sticking out, and showed it to him.

He laughed so suddenly, he snorted. "Really?"

I nodded. "Don't be so surprised. This is tame."

"So if you came here by yourself, how many of those post-its would you use?"

"Maybe half a pad."

"And is this the only library where you do this?"

"No. I'll go to libraries all over the city. Sometimes, I'll go to libraries in colleges or universities."

"And it makes you feel alive?" he asked.

I picked up the next book. It was a fantasy novel. On the teddy bear, I wrote, "Do you fantasize about walking?"

"Pretty snarky," Fletch commented when he looked at it.

I offered him the pen. "Do you want to give it a try?"

He accepted the pad of teddy bears and selected the next book from the stack. It was a murder mystery. "I suppose it would be obvious to write, 'It was the butler.'"

"Are you going to write the obvious thing?"

He scribbled something and showed me the note before he put it inside the book. It read, "It was the investigator. No one suspects the investigator."

"Brilliant."

Chapter Five
Triangle

Fletch

A cop was approaching us. Shannon had told me beforehand all about what she did when cops questioned her.

She put her finger in the air and said, "The first rule for the effective vandal is to do it at dusk."

"Why dusk?"

"My lies sound way better with a bit of light on me. I always carry a camera with me and I do my art next to a fairly prominent piece. If a cop approaches me, I ditch my supplies and pretend to be taking pictures of a more famous piece of vandalism than what I've made."

"Sounds suspicious," I yawned. "What if you get paint on your hands or your clothes?"

"I always carry latex gloves and yes, it would be terrible if I got fresh paint on my outfit. It's never happened," she said sternly.

"Don't the cops find your stash of paint cans, gloves, and whatever?"

She smiled wickedly. "They *never* have."

"Why not?"

"Because they are always so distracted by me that they don't look. I'll talk to them about the piece I'm taking pictures of, show them the pictures I've taken already, show them my blog, which is nothing but various pieces of vandalism throughout the city. Lots of the patrolling officers know me by name. They'll talk to me for a few minutes and then they'll get called away before they can even check to see if the paint on the wall is dry."

I snorted. "You can't be that charming."

She shrugged her shoulders. "Come with me and I'll show you how charming I can be."

That was how I ended up in an abandoned alleyway in the downtown core, squatting in a corner while she wrote various n words in a line, "Narcissism. Necrophilia. Nihilism. Nepotism. Narcolepsy. Nefelibata."

I found it interesting in a weird way. She dumped her supplies before I had even realized a cop had entered the alley and was approaching us. She was on her face on the cement taking a picture of a broken heart with arrows sticking out in all directions that had been spray-painted half on the building and half on the ground.

When Shannon stood up and showed me the pictures, I was impressed. The angle she got would make the photograph a stunning addition to her blog and the quality of the shot added to her credibility with the cop.

"What's going on here?" the cop asked firmly as he approached us.

She turned to him. "Hi, Todd. How's it going?"

He put away the flashlight he had been shining at us. "Fine. Fine. And how's it going with you?"

She smiled at Officer Todd and showed him the pictures she had just shown me, and it played out exactly the way she said it would.

I was gobsmacked as she entertained him until he got a call that he had to leave. She walked with him out of the alley and beckoned for me to follow them. There was more graffiti on the street outside and she attempted to get more pictures as Officer Todd went on his way. Once he was out of sight, she went back and got her supplies.

"Have you ever lost your bag?" I asked.

"Happens all the time. I'm making a bag that looks like moss on one side so I can hide my stuff and I don't have to worry about someone taking it before I come back. One time, I had to leave three spray cans and when I came back, the spray cans had been used and some thoughtless dickbrain had mucked up my piece. I got the idea for the bag from a friend of mine who likes to hide things in disposable diapers that look like they've been crapped in, but have merely been smeared with chocolate."

Before I knew it, she'd found me a wall to make a mark on. She handed me some gloves and a can of blue paint.

I stared at her. "I don't know what to do."

"Something to commemorate our date?" she suggested.

My brain was empty. Since I knew I couldn't do something stylish, I opted to do something meaningful.

"We've got about ten minutes until sundown."

I sprayed a triangle, like the one I'd played during the ballet.

I thought it was stupid, but she looked pleased. "For your first try, that was great. Full of meaning, it was. Let's go." She put everything in a backpack she strapped to my shoulders.

Chapter Six
The Goddess of Social Media

Fletch

On Monday, I looked at my social media. The most likes I had ever received for a photo was for a post where I was swinging bells for 'A Carol of Bells' at Christmas. I got forty-two for that post. Most people did not want to support my orchestra. They were my age and anything else was preferable to them. I got twenty likes from my closest friends whenever I posted anything, but I had hundreds of friends on Facebook and they mostly refrained from commenting on whatever I was doing… until Shannon tagged me in a picture.

What followed was an unholy outpouring of interest.

In the picture, we were sitting at a bus stop. She had her legs over my lap and her arm around my neck. My arm was around her waist. We had a pair of earbuds strung from my phone with one in her ear and one in mine. We wore sunglasses and blew huge bubbles of blue bubble gum. The two of us were such an outburst of color and life, I wasn't sure if anyone noticed that she had vandalized the wall behind us with a heavy-duty pen. It read, "The purpose of our lives is to love one another."

It had a hundred and twenty likes.

As I scanned through the names, Simon's was there. He had given it a WOW emoji, which meant he hadn't liked it. Further down, a collection of my ex-girlfriends had weighed in. All were overly eager to wish me well.

Shannon and I had spent the entire day together, taking pictures and getting to know each other. For me, it was becoming clearer and clearer why every man was in love with her. She was unpredictable. On our date, she had taken a marker and written on my forearm, "Mine."

I had been really excited, feeling my heart hammer in my chest. How badly did I want to be hers?

She hesitated and then wrote, "Field" after it.

She was a love rollercoaster.

"Ever think of getting a tattoo?" I asked her.

"I don't want to mark myself. I want to mark everything else," she replied.

Aside from the kiss I pressed her into on our first date, I tried my best not to appear overeager. Her job was to eat my heart and I had been a fool to think she wasn't good at it. I had to think of a strategy to get her to say that she wanted to be my girlfriend, but for the time being my brain was blank. I had never tried to be the male equivalent of what she was. I didn't know how to make a woman want me so much she couldn't think.

One thing was certain, she wanted connection, but I knew from experience with other artists that she didn't want a connection with just anybody. She wanted a connection with someone who gave her something she could not get anywhere else.

Being in the orchestra did not pay all my bills. As a matter of fact, it did not pay most of them. When I played for the orchestra, I was often paid in honorariums. I also did odd one-shots where I was paid for covering for other musicians. On a normal workday, I put in hours at a music store, selling sheet music and giving musical demonstrations to parents who were renting instruments for their children. For my fourth side hustle, I constructed specialty xylophones and sold them online.

Giving seven hundred dollars to Natalie for the opportunity of being handcuffed to Shannon had been insanely excessive. Normally, I was frugal to a fault. I hadn't known that dating Shannon would be the crown of my romantic history.

Thinking back, Natalie had thought she killed Shannon after she hit her over the head. Natalie was screaming and swearing. I called to her and asked her to bring Shannon into the camp kitchen so I could confirm whether or not she was dead, since Natalie was too deranged to know if something was dead or alive. After checking her pulse, I comforted Natalie, saying Shannon would be fine. At that moment, something about the unconscious girl's face had struck me as familiar. I asked Natalie who she was.

"She's Shannon Bilx," Natalie had told me.

The rest was history. I told her about my cousin, Simon, and convinced her to calm down, give me the keys, take the money and leave without looking back.

Reminiscing, I had seen a different photo of Shannon almost every week for over two years. Even when I thought everything was great between her and Simon, I had been curious about her. Secretly, I had wanted to meet her, wondered why Simon had been able to win her, felt sorry for him when things with her hadn't gone his way, and hoped there was a woman like that on my horizon. Her appeal was everywhere. She made everything shine.

What did a girl who saw beauty in dirty alleyways want?

Chapter Seven
The Jewelry Box

Shannon

The first time I toured my apartment, I gasped at its small size and said, "If I move here, I might as well be living in my jewelry box."

I had looked at the place, rolling the situation of my new life around in my head. First, I could not go home. Second, I could not go back to the dorms at the college. Third, I did not want a roommate.

I had to accept that I was responsible for myself and if I was going to manage that, then I needed to choose a home I could afford.

I signed the lease and slowly started making the place over to look like a jewelry box. That was accomplished by combining elements from my enormous jewelry box from back when I was still the queen of everything. I started by hanging pink velvet curtains. I hung mirrors and brought in the plushest furniture I could afford. I decorated the drapes in gold trim and hung crystals everywhere I could.

When my dates visited my apartment, they had a collection of thoughts that were easy to read.

"This is a girl's apartment."

"I've never been in such a girly apartment."

"I could never live in a place like this. No man could live in a place like this."

"Wait. This couch is comfortable."

"All these cushions make me feel right at home. Maybe all this pink isn't so bad."

"I wonder if her bed is comfortable."

Sometimes, I would catch them sneaking a peek into the closet off the living room that was so large I had tucked my bed inside. Some of the other tenants in the building had their beds out in the open, or they slept on a couch that transformed into a bed and used the closet to store their mountain bike. I did not own a mountain bike, and nor would I allow guests to lounge where I intended to sleep later.

The kitchen had been the hardest part to decorate. The cupboards were garbage, so I covered them in gold patterned contact paper. All my dishes were clear, even if they weren't crystal, except for my utensils which were gold. I had pink placemats. The fridge looked terrible, so did the microwave, but I couldn't live entirely in a jewelry box. Still, I shook my head at that fridge. My toilet was prettier.

My dates who visited did not know what it would mean for the rest of their lives if they decided to partner up with a woman who decorated her apartment the way I did. They were confused. They wanted to be with an attractive woman, a feminine woman, a woman who presented the way I did when I was on their arm. They looked at their surroundings in my apartment and they wondered what they would have to sacrifice if they decided on me.

Sometimes they'd talk to me about it. "So, are you married to this style of decorating?"

I'd smirk and let them believe there wasn't much more to me than what they could see.

Then they'd tell me about how they would like to see their future house decorated. They'd describe a hunting lodge, or a dark library, or the very clean lines of stainless steel appliances. Unfortunately for my morale, I agreed with that one. I did not have the appliances I had because I had chosen them.

It was obvious that most of these men had never even thought about interior design before. I was inadvertently forcing them to think about the future. Both the future for that evening (about whether or not he could stand to hang out in a pink velvet parlor) and the far future of the rest of their lives (if he could stand pink drapes as part of a compromise). Sometimes men stood in the entryway on the other side of my crystal beaded curtain and wondered if there was a reward for tolerating this new side of me.

I had not invited Fletch over to my apartment yet. I knew why I hadn't. If he came in and thought all those things the other men thought, I didn't know if I would be able to stand it.

That was the moment I knew…

That I liked Fletch more than I had ever liked anyone.

Chapter Eight
Sorrowful Natalie

Shannon

The next time I saw Natalie, she was not coming to the recording studio to sing. She had an overdue bill for recording time she'd used, and she was completely unable to pay it. Levi, my boss, had arranged for her to do some voice-overs to pay the bill.

She came in, looking far less fabulous than normal. Her yellow hair had weird bends in it because it had not been properly straightened. Her expression made the cleft in her chin look weak instead of powerful—a bad sign.

I greeted her like I hadn't spent months with her crabbing about the toughness of the music industry, and sent her directly to the back.

I popped in a bit later and watched Natalie shift her weight on a stool as she read.

Next to me, Levi asked, "Are you seeing someone lately?" He never asked me questions like that. I saw it as a red flag.

"Did you have someone in mind?" I asked.

"My nephew, Adam, wanted me to find out for him."

"You can tell him that I'm in a hot new relationship and I am hardly coming up for air these days," I said dryly.

Levi sniggered. "Is that true?"

"Yup," I said like a nearly dead fish blowing a bubble.

"What's the truth?" he persisted.

I took a deep breath, remembered that I had worked for Levi for four years and I had always found him to be the least sleazy man I had ever met. There was no reason to cut him off without giving him a hint as to which way the wind was blowing. "I am seeing someone new. It's been going well. I don't want to jinx it, since I have a good feeling about him." I cleared my throat and changed the subject. "I was going to tell you that I had an extremely rough encounter with Natalie the other night and something happened that has cooled my enthusiasm for supporting her singing career."

Levi frowned deeply. "Shannon, everyone has a hard time making it in this business and if our people go far, it's much better for our studio."

"She hit me," I explained.

"Did you hit her?"

I shook my head in the negative.

"You didn't even get one punch in?" he asked.

"I couldn't. I was knocked out."

Levi was understandably stunned.

"I didn't report her to the police for assault and I'm not going to. I don't think she'll do anything like that again because I'm not going to be around her. I'm not going to stop you from working with her or quit working with you if you do. I'm just telling you what happened so you can understand why I've cooled and why I plan to stay cool. I'll get back to the front."

He stopped me before I could head out. "Are you sure you don't want to tell me more about this?"

"Yup. I thought she was my friend. She's not. I won't be mixing business with friendship again."

He nodded and let me go back to my desk.

I plugged numbers into my calculator and then into the spreadsheets on my computer until lunchtime. Levi and Natalie finished their work and migrated to the front. At that moment, Adam came in the front door.

I hardly looked up.

Adam had lunch with Levi often enough that his arrival was not sensational.

I was not attracted to him. The problem with him was that he was the personification of the men I usually dated and they were all the same. I didn't need to do any digging to find out what he was thinking; his thoughts were all over his face. It made him the very opposite of Fletch. Normally, I would have let a man like Adam take me out, spend some money on me, but lately… since meeting Fletch, the idea bored me.

Adam invited Levi to lunch and since Natalie was standing next to him, he invited her too. Levi hadn't had a chance to tell Adam that his attention would be unwelcome, so he approached my desk and asked me if I wanted to go to lunch with them.

"I'm sorry," I said with a practiced flippant smile. "I can't today. I have so much work to finish."

Levi interrupted. "She's been taking off early the last few nights, seeing a new man. She needs to play catchup, so let's head out. I don't have all day for a lunch break."

It was a lie, but it worked double time, both giving an excuse and the reason why I wouldn't be available later.

I sighed a breath of relief as the three of them left the office. We were closed during lunch hour so I locked the door behind them.

Then, I did the thing I did every day during lunch break. I didn't eat. I had a bed under the reception desk that I unrolled during lunch hour. My hobbies kept me up late at night or got me up early in the morning. If I didn't sleep during the hour I had for lunch, I wouldn't be able to work a whole day. I usually had a snack at my desk in the afternoon and Levi had never complained that I sometimes munched on carrot sticks as I crunched numbers.

That day, however, it took me an extra few minutes to calm down. It was hard to say exactly what bothered me so much about seeing Natalie. She hadn't done or said anything to me. She'd come in and read a few lines for a few bucks. Perhaps she looked sad that we weren't friends anymore.

Chapter Nine
Tear off the Number

Shannon

Fletch looked at the advertisements I'd made.

"Don't you like them?" I asked with a wicked smile.

His eyes flicked over the page. "Well, it's an ad for babysitting. But it looks like it's not a teenage girl looking to earn some extra cash, but an alien from outer space trying to study humans with appalling spelling."

"Yup."

"Need someone to wantch your younglings with great interst? Look no futer than Sarah Delta. She will protect your baby. Low fees. Will wantch your baby in the safety of ur own home. Accepts cash. Saves younglings from choking, wallowing in poison, and cooking with the stove. Call now for FREEze estimate. I, Sarah Delta, will come to u." Fletch swallowed a laugh. "And we're going to staple these to power poles?"

"Yup!"

"The alien watermark in the background really sells it, and all these rippable number tags on the bottom. Whose phone number is this anyway?"

"It's a rejection hotline number," I explained.

"It's what?"

I smiled. "It's a fake number me and my lady friends give out to men when a man will not stop hounding us for our number. He takes the fake number and shoves off, much to our relief, and then later he calls it and hears a very nice recording about how the woman who gave him that number does not want to see him."

"There is such a thing?"

"Of course there is, honey," I said condescendingly as I pinched his cheek. "You're just such a nice guy that you've never been given that number… or one like it." I let go of him. "I could have given the poster a different number. There's one where the recording tells you that you have bad breath and another one that says you have something stuck in your teeth over and over."

"But you picked the rejection line?" Fletch asked, trailing after me on the sidewalk.

"Yup."

"Why?"

"To spread the news that such a hotline exists. Anyone who calls it will never forget it. I'm not one to say that only chicks need numbers like this. If a man needs one and he's curious enough to call our phone number, he'll learn all about it." I shook my hair merrily. "It's my way of making the world a bit brighter with a double whammy. First, whoever reads the ad will certainly be entertained and then if they call the number, they'll get smarter too. They can even rip off the number and keep it with them in their bag, giving it away immediately to any creep who won't stop hounding them for their digits."

Fletch followed me with the staple gun and I let him staple the ads to the poles while I looked at what else was posted. The first few poles were boring, but the fourth one had an ad that caught my attention.

I read it. "Does your dog or cat exhibit any of the following symptoms? Barking or meowing? Ruining furniture? Peeing on your bed or in other unwanted areas? Your pet is sexually frustrated! Call Carver Criche, an expert at jerking pets off."

I gasped. What had Natalie done? I whipped out my phone and did a reverse lookup on the number she'd provided for him. When the screen loaded, it showed that it was an unlisted number. It was not a prank number like the one I was using for my ad. It had to be his real phone number. There was even a picture of him in black and white on the ad. I loaded in Facebook and found the picture she'd stolen off his company's Facebook page.

Fletcher finished stapling and came over to see what I was looking at. "Carver Criche?" he said incredulously. "Think your friend, Natalie, did this?"

"Of course. This is the kind of thing we liked doing together. I mean, I didn't know she would do up a flyer herself, but this is the sort of thing she and I used to share on Pinterest when we were still friends." I stared at the paper in horror.

"It's not a good joke," Fletch said, tearing it clean off the pole.

I sighed in mild relief. "Even if we pull down the ones we find, we still probably won't get them all."

He nodded. "Yeah, but we got this one."

Fletch put his arm around me, I slipped my arm around him, and together we walked to the next pole, where there was another ad that had to be torn down.

Chapter Ten
Hide your Butterflies

Shannon

Fletch walked me home. "I promise you, wherever I go, whatever I do, I'll keep an eye out for those ads on the power poles and if I see any more of them, I'll pull them down."

"Thanks," I said, looking over the crumpled, torn ads in my hands. "I feel like I must be missing something. Sure, Natalie was angry at Carver for promising her a contract and then always forgetting the papers, or putting her off with some other excuse. Something about this doesn't make sense."

"What?"

"Why did Natalie think you were Carver? From the picture on this flyer, it seems pretty clear to me that you don't look that much like him. If she knew him so well... if she had been fighting with him, then why did she mistake you for him?"

"It was dark? She was a little drunk?" Fletch supplied.

"It was dark," I agreed. "I don't know if she'd been drinking. Couldn't have been that much, because she didn't smell like a sewer rat. You know, as I think it over, I think the truth might be something else."

"Like what?"

"That she was lying about what he was doing to her. Maybe she didn't know him very well, at all. Maybe that was why she had to hit me over the head with the brick. She needed me to help with the kidnapping, but she didn't want me there for the

interrogation, because she was going to use the kidnapping as a
way to *get* to know him. She needed to get rid of me."

Fletch kissed the spot on my head where my goose egg had
been. "You think your fight with her was a part of her plan?
That she staged it?"

I nodded. "Yeah, and this ad means she's still trying to get
his attention, but I don't see how this kind of thing could bring
positive attention. This could only bring righteous indignation
down on her head, maybe even a lawsuit. I don't know why
she'd want to risk it, but I don't know how many things she's
tried before."

We were at my door.

"Do you want me to come up with you?" Fletch offered, his
hand cupped around my ear as if he whispered a secret to me.

I thought about the rooms I had not yet shown him—the
jewelry box. "Maybe not tonight," I said, touching his hands
and arms because I liked it so much when he touched me. "I
need to do some thinking, and I may have already had the
stuffing knocked out of me today."

"All the more reason why I should come up. I'll rub your
feet and take care of you." His voice was tantalizing as his
words floated across the air to me.

I decided to lay the honest reason down between us. "I'm not
ready to show you my place. We need to meet out in the open a
few more times. I have a couple more *projects* on my mind for
this week and the week after. I'm not trying to disguise myself,
I would just feel more comfortable showing you the inside of
my home after we've played together in the streets a few more

times. Can you wait a bit longer? Or maybe we should go to your place?"

He immediately straightened. "When you put it that way, I agree with you completely."

I caught on. "You don't want to show me your place either?"

He grinned. It was the type of grin that made you want to forgive the next thing he said no matter what it was. "No. I don't." He took my hand in his and rubbed the back of it with his thumb. "Even though you've been so generous as to tell me what you like when it's illegal, I would like to put my best foot forward with you. I didn't think I needed to vacuum, but I can see now that I do. I probably need to do a few other things too. Forgive me." He kissed the back of my hand. "The goal is not to impress you, but to refrain from disgusting you."

I patted him on the arm. "You don't know that I'm not the sort of girl who falls asleep in dill pickle potato chip crumbs."

He laughed like that was the biggest joke of the night. "I'll bring some the next time I come by. You should have a supply if they make your hips look like that." He kissed the side of my head. "I'll see you later."

I watched him let me go, grab hold of the railing to my entrance, leap over the rail and the bush on the other side of it. He disappeared a heartbeat later. It was already after dark and anything that wasn't illuminated by the light over my head was cast in a thick shadow.

I opened the door to my apartment building and stopped in front of my mailbox. I took out my key and opened it. I hardly noticed that a person, all in black, had come down the stairwell and into the atrium. I didn't turn to look at that person until I felt the barrel of a gun in my shoulder blade.

I froze.

"Come quietly and you won't get hurt," a man's voice said.

Chapter Eleven
Simon Said

Fletch

I looked at the likes. There were almost two hundred likes on the photograph. It was a picture of me kissing Shannon. It was from a date we'd had a few days ago. I had pushed her up against a brick wall in the inner city. We'd had an absolutely delicious makeout session and I had been so involved, I hadn't noticed her taking out her phone or her taking pictures of us.

It was an incredibly sexy picture. I was really into kissing her and all that vulnerability of what a man looks like when he's in love was showing.

Her face was a puzzle. She was trying to match my enthusiasm, but she was also trying to take the picture. She had a selfie stick. I knew she had it on her that night. Before we'd gone on our date that was half dinner and half defacing the city street, she'd asked me if it was okay for her to post any really good pictures of us on her social media accounts. I said it was fine. The last picture she'd taken of us had been a big hit and this one was an even bigger hit, except that I didn't like that she'd put that little piece of my soul on the internet for my mum, my coworkers, and Simon to see.

Simon was seething. I went home to see my parents after my poster date with Shannon and he was over visiting my younger brother, Finn, who still lived at home.

"What did you do?" he asked without saying hello.

"Hmm?"

"What did you do to make Shannon Bilx fall in love with you?"

I rubbed the back of my neck. "I didn't do anything. She's not in love with me. We were just fooling around."

I said that last line just in time for my mother to hear me say it. "I don't like the idea of you fooling around with anyone, and posting it on the internet is just tasteless."

At that moment, I realized another reason why it was in Shannon's best interest not to tell her dates what she was really like. There was no way their mothers would approve of a woman like her, and if she kept her mouth shut, she could easily slide under their radar without rousing their open disapproval.

It was at that moment that I realized that Shannon must really like me. She had posted that picture in order to bring everything out in the open. If I couldn't handle the blowback after a tiny picture of us kissing, there was no way I could handle the pressure of being her man.

I turned back to my mother and tried again for an explanation. "I shouldn't have said we were fooling around, mum. I was kissing her. We're dating. It's just a bit awkward to talk about when Simon used to date her before me."

My mum immediately jumped on Simon. "You used to date her? What kind of a girl is she?"

I also wanted to hear his answer.

"She's crabby," he responded. "She doesn't like anything. She doesn't say what she's thinking, and she's a tease." Soon he petered out, not sure how to bash her.

"Do you feel like she's teasing you, Fletch?" my mum asked.

I shrugged. "I'm hardly a prize, mum. I'm sure Shannon could find a fancier man to hang out with if she wanted to boost her ego. She's really exciting. She could have anyone."

Simon snorted.

"What I mean to say is… it might not work out with her, but I don't think she's playing with me just to have another scalp on her belt. So far, all that's happened is that we enjoy being together."

"Is she as crabby as Simon says?"

"She just has clear boundaries about what she's willing to talk about. That's all. Some things are nobody's business."

"Hmm…" Mum hummed. "She sounds like trouble. How could you trust someone who tells you some things are none of your business when she goes ahead and posts a picture like that? She's careful with her own privacy, but not yours?"

"Exactly," Simon chimed in.

I scoffed. "It's not important today when I've only gone on a handful of dates with her. She's not my girlfriend even. She could even be seeing other guys for all I know, and for now, that's fine. I don't own her."

"Then you don't mind if I set you up on a date with someone?" my mum asked tentatively.

"It might be better to wait if you want it to work out."

"Why? If she's not your girlfriend?"

I glanced at Simon, who was staring coldly at me.

If Simon had not been standing there, I would have told my mother that it didn't matter what woman she set me up with, I wouldn't like her. Next to Shannon, she would look like a sad replacement, and I didn't think it was right to put someone at that kind of disadvantage.

I brushed off any discomfort I was feeling, the same way I had seen Shannon do it. "I'll take out whoever you want, mum."

Simon was staring at me. We had known each other all our lives, but he had never looked at me that way before. "You're doing it!"

"I'm doing what?"

"You're acting like her! Classic Shannon! That's exactly the way Shannon acts when she'd rather not talk about it. Later tonight, auntie, you'll get a text from him saying he's changed his mind, but he won't be here for you to interrogate."

My mother chuckled. "That may be 'classic Shannon', but it is also 'classic Fletcher!' If you must know, I do it too." She patted me on the cheek. "Let me know if you want me to set you up."

"Right. Thanks."

She wandered away from relieved me and stunned Simon.

Later, when I was on my way out, he stopped me. "Fletch… seriously… what did you do to get her to notice you?"

"What do you mean?"

"You had to have *done* something. We're not that different. How could she fall for you and not me?"

I brushed off my clothes and took a deep breath. "I told you. She's not in love with me. She's trying me out."

"That picture is her 'trying you out'?" he gaped in amazement. She had never tried him out.

"Does it bother you that I'm dating her?" One look at Simon and I saw that I shouldn't have asked. Of course, it bothered him. "It might turn out to be nothing," I amended.

He scowled.

"Look, I met her because of what you told me about her. I'm sorry, but I was curious and I wanted to get to know more about her. You know how different she is from other women. I liked what I saw, kissed her when I felt like it, listened to her when she talked, and she liked being listened to… so she talked more. I kissed her more and she posted that picture on the internet."

"You kissed her when you felt like it? And she *let* you?" he growled.

"Yes."

"That simply?"

"Yes," I repeated, my patience wearing thin. "But she's not my girlfriend or anything. For all I know, she's out with someone else right now."

"She's going to rip out your heart," he warned.

I did see where he was going with that, and honestly, I didn't think he was wrong. I thought about patting him on the head and spewing some crappy speech about how dating was a journey and each person you dated was another stepping stone to prepare you for the person you were meant to be with. I also considered turning to him and mouthing off some other crap about how she was likely to dump me before the weekend, but I didn't think that was true either.

Instead, I turned to him and said, "She told me why it didn't work out with you."

His eyes narrowed. "She did?"

"Yeah. She told me that you were a great guy, but that she had nothing in common with you and didn't want to bring you into her world when there was so little the two of you shared."

"And you're so different from me?" he gasped. "We're basically the same."

"Stop," I said, putting my hands on both his shoulders. "She liked you. That means a lot about what a good person you are, but she's not for you. You just didn't want to hear it, but I think you knew it too. You're going to have to take the valentine and go home."

Simon knocked my hands off him. He started heading back up the stairs to the kitchen when he abruptly turned around. "I want you to call me when it doesn't work out. Whatever time of day or night, I want you to call me the moment she tells you that she can't be with you. Can you do that for me?"

I nodded. "I guess."

"I'll have some advice for you when that happens."

He walked away, but I called after him, "Can't wait to hear it!"

Chapter Twelve
Inside the Jewelry Box

Shannon

I would have liked to have fought him harder, but there was something strange about him, and the way he ordered me around. I wasn't as brave as Fletch, in that I did not look over my shoulder and smile at my abductor, but I did manage a glance over my shoulder. The man's face was mostly covered in a scarf, he wore a fedora on his head, and he smelled like sugar cookies.

If I hadn't seen Fletch jump over the hedge and head home, I would have thought he was pulling a prank on me.

The man ordered me through the doors and up the stairs.

"You smell good," I said, breaking the ice as cleverly as a child.

"Move," he said, trying to sound gruff and failing.

"Do I know you?" I continued, thinking that I knew dozens of men who would love to date me, and maybe one of them got up the courage to plan something like this. I couldn't see him well enough to recognize him and his voice did not sound familiar.

"I don't know, do you?" he said, pushing the barrel of his gun into my back.

"Why do you smell yummy? A kidnapper shouldn't smell yummy. It totally gives off the wrong vibe. Aren't you supposed to smell like B.O. and latex?"

"Been kidnapped a lot, have you?"

"I've been pranked a lot," I admitted, turning the corner in the stairs to arrive on my floor.

"This isn't a prank," he hissed, letting me feel the gun again. "Open the door."

I stood in front of the door, fumbled with my keys, and wondered what I ought to do next. To go into the apartment and allow him inside with me seemed crazy. I pretended to juggle the objects in my arms to buy time while I asked him, "What do you want?"

"I want to talk to you."

"Can't we do that out here?"

He snatched the keys out of my hand, unlocked the door, and pushed me inside. My apartment was puny, and right beside the door was my couch. With one push, the flyers in my hands fell to the floor, and he handcuffed me to a tall lamp I had placed next to the couch. Then he stepped away from me and removed his scarf, allowing it to fall fashionably around his neck.

It was Carver Criche.

I wouldn't have known him if I didn't have half a dozen flyers with his face printed on them strewn all over my floor. His eyebrows were dark brown and his eyes were a watered-down blue. His bone structure made him look older and more respectable than he deserved. He was probably close to the same age as Fletch, but Fletch's light bones and cartilage made him look younger.

Carver bent and picked up one of the flyers. Stroking it between his fingers, he waved it under my nose. "Why are you defaming me by hanging these up around town?"

"I'm not. I was taking them down," I replied, whacking my handcuff against the lamp. It didn't make the proper sound. It thudded instead of clanked. It was supposed to be so loud, it woke the neighbors.

"Stop that," he commanded through clenched teeth, pointing the gun at me. "This will go so much better if you simply answer me. When I'm finished, I'll take off the handcuffs and leave."

The lamp next to me shone light onto the handcuff that lay limply around the stem of the lamp. I leaned over and examined it. "There are teeth marks in this."

He turned off the lamp. "You're a lot less fun than you look," he commented sourly. "If you were taking down the flyers, then could you explain to me why you'd do that?"

I exhaled. I didn't want to explain anything. I didn't want to talk about Natalie and why she was doing what she was doing. "They just looked hateful," I hedged.

He didn't say anything for a moment, looking at me like half of him didn't want to talk to me and the other half wanted to talk to me desperately.

I started sniffing the air. "Why do you smell like cookie dough?"

"Okay! You wrenched it out of me," he exclaimed like he was the one in handcuffs and not me. "I saw you kidnap that guy." He was trying to distract me.

I yawned. "I don't remember kidnapping anyone."

"No. I saw you outside the tour bus that night. The drummer from the other band left the bus, got two steps away before I heard you and your friend say my name and cart him away."

I eyed him warily. "What happened after that?"

"I followed you."

I gawked in disbelief. "What did you see?"

"I saw the campground. I saw you and your friend fighting. I saw her clock you with a brick, drag you into the camp kitchen and drive away."

Pouting my lips playfully, I asked, "And you followed her as she drove away and didn't come to help me?"

He nodded. "There was no point in going in after you… you weren't going anywhere. She'd handcuffed you to that guy."

"Where did she go?" I asked, the chuckle bubbling up from my chest. "What did she do?"

He stuttered, too excited to keep his voice smooth. "I-it wasn't very remarkable. She drove to a few houses. It looked like she was dropping off money. Then she went to a drive-thru and ended up at a man's house who let her in like he didn't like the sight of her, but she was better than his pillow."

"And then?" I egged him on.

"Then, I drove back to the camp kitchen, but you and the drummer were gone."

"Do you know my friend? Is that why you followed her?"

"No. I'd never seen her before in my life."

"Okay, that makes sense," I said as I moved my arm around in the uncomfortable handcuff. I looked at it again, only to see that the silver sheen of the metal was coming off on the sleeve of my coat. "I knew it!" I barked before I bent over and bit the handcuff in half. I spit the cookie into a decorative dish on my coffee table and stood up.

He sighed. "You've seen them before? Handcuffs made out of cookies."

"They're very convincing," I said, eying his gun, which was also a cookie. "Where did you get them?"

"A friend gave them to me. They've been sitting in my car for weeks. Very smart of you not to eat it."

I broke the other one off the lamp without biting it and I had to hand it to the baker, it was harder to break than made sense for a cookie. I held the broken pieces in my hands. The icing work was exquisite. "How much did these cost?"

He shrugged. "I have no idea. They were a gift. I only decided to use them tonight as a way to meet you because I saw you tearing down those posters. Are you going to tell me about why you and your friend were going to kidnap me and why these posters have appeared around town?"

I waffled, thinking about what I ought to tell him. "I don't want to be involved in this anymore."

"Then why did you tear the posters down?" he demanded.

"Because I don't think *you* should be involved in this anymore either. If you go digging into this, you're not going to find anything you want to know about. Ask the bump on my head."

He wetted his teeth. "I'm dying of curiosity."

"You should ignore this stuff," I advised, pinching up leftover crumbs.

When I raised my head, I was immediately arrested by the languid way in which he regarded me from across the room. I only had one thought, and that was that this guy wasn't interested in discovering who Natalie was or why she was interested in him. He followed Natalie that night because he believed she was running a quick errand and would soon be back at the camp kitchen. It had ruined his night's entertainment that she didn't come back and that Fletch and I were gone by the time he returned. He wanted to understand what was going on, but more than that, he wanted to get to know me. That was why he was standing in my apartment instead of Fletch's or Natalie's.

"I'll call the police for you," I said, pulling my phone out of my coat pocket.

"Wait! No!" he exclaimed, stepping toward me.

"Why?" I asked, hesitating. "I know the cops well and they can easily pick the posters off the poles while they're patrolling. What's the big deal?"

"Oh," he said, lowering his shoulders. "I thought you were going to report that I'd kidnapped you."

"With a cookie?" I droned. "It wouldn't have held me. I have been tolerating you only because you introduced yourself to me immediately and I agree you have reason to speak to me. Otherwise, I would have busted your face. This place is full of heavy glass."

He leaned against my faux mantelpiece that displayed two large glass sculptures. "Wouldn't you be more worried about what a man in your apartment could do to you?"

I raised my eyebrows like he bored me and looked at my phone. "I have a gun and I can throw it pretty hard." I finished dialing the police and the phone rang at the police station, where it was answered by Officer Todd.

I explained the situation, sent Todd a picture of the flyers I'd pulled down, said that Carver was in my apartment, and he was most unhappy about the defamation.

Todd laughed on the other end of the phone. "Have you ever thought about being a police officer, Shannon? I'm not sure anyone knows the streets better than you."

From that point on, I engaged in some extremely heavy flirting with Officer Todd and ignored Carver completely. I hoped he would get the hint that he and I were done talking and he should leave on his own. I also hoped that Todd would clue into how uncomfortable I was with Carver in my apartment without me having to spell it out for him.

Unfortunately, Carver seemed to enjoy listening to me flirt. He made himself comfortable in a chair and listened to my end of the conversation. He smiled, laughed, and made eyes at me like everything I said was for him.

Finally, Todd had to answer a call. That was what always happened whenever I ran into a cop. Eventually, they always had to go. I ended the call unhappily and stared at my unwanted guest. "Was there something else you needed?"

"Your phone number?" he asked, raising his eyebrows like he knew he was asking a lot.

I smiled and said, "Of course." I ripped a number off one of the posters I had made and offered it to him.

He reached for it, but I pulled it back. "I'll give this to you, but you have to promise to leave right after. I'm tired. It's been a long day, and I require some privacy."

He took the number and left, as obedient as a dog.

When he called the number, he would get the message that told him that the woman who gave him her number did not like him, and wanted to let him down in the kindest way possible.

Chapter Thirteen
Dinner of Gems

Fletch

No matter where I looked, there were no more posters advertising Carver, the pervert petter. I was tired of looking for them when I went to work a week later. I hadn't seen Shannon since that night, though she texted often. I tried to call her a time or two, but I always got a text back that said it wasn't a good time. She was preparing for something and I'd just have to wait.

My boss at the music store, Turner, called to me as I came in. "You got a letter," he said, handing me an envelope.

I took it. It looked like a wedding invitation as it was printed on pink hand-pressed paper. I couldn't think of who I knew who was still sending out physical wedding invitations when I looked at the return address. It was Shannon's.

"Who's getting married?" Turner asked me from the other side of the counter.

"If this is a wedding invitation, I'll eat it," I said sourly as I broke the red wax seal on the back. Flipping it open, I read the contents.

"What is it?"

"It's an invitation."

"To what? An opera troupe party?" Turner asked.

"No. It's an invitation for a dinner date from a woman I have been seeing," I explained.

"Anyone I know?" he asked, bending to look inside.

"No."

"Is she that hottie you were making out with against the wall?" he sniggered.

I didn't groan or whine. The guy who did that was a skin I had shed recently. Instead of rebuffing the jab, I just looked at him. No contempt. Not even a desire to defend myself. Not even the urge to tell him how amazing it had felt to kiss her. I didn't even stoop to say, "You wouldn't understand." I folded the invitation up and slid it into my pocket. "I'll get to work putting out the new sheet music, shall I?"

Turner didn't apologize or ask me to tell him more about Shannon. He just let it go. I had never known him to do that. Working in a music store didn't have many pleasures, teasing me was probably the most fun he had at work. Though I did hear him sit down at one of the pianos and play before his lunch break. His longing was palpable through the music.

The moment I realized he was jealous was a strange one. The thing was, the makeout session against a filthy brick wall was on the other side of the spectrum from a dainty pink dinner invitation. No one got it all from one woman. Shannon was attempting it anyway. As if the purpose of life was to experience the highest high love could give. That was how Shannon organized herself. But who was a gift like that for?

An odd sensation rippled through me as I sang the alphabet song to help with the filing and I saw Shannon through Turner's eyes.

***

As soon as I walked through the door to Shannon's apartment, I knew what was going on.

"You're using me," I said, making my expression deadpan as I looked her over.

The dress she was wearing probably wasn't the most expensive one she owned. It was the one that made her look the most beautiful. It was part of the whole experience she was creating. The dress was mauve and black. Mauve satin and black ribbon, her clothes hugging and pinching her in all the right places. Her makeup was so artfully done, she almost didn't look human.

"What am I trying to do?" she asked giddily, a touch of deep crimson on each of her cheeks.

"You got your perfect date outside. This is your perfect date at home. You've been setting the stage for days? Maybe the whole week we haven't seen each other?"

She leaned toward me with stars in her eyes. "Maybe my whole life."

I thought she was going to kiss me, but instead, she licked the tip of my nose and led me deeper into the apartment.

The place was tiny. It was like she'd rented two parking spaces and built an apartment around them. The walls were covered with mirrors and other reflective art to try to conceal how little space there was. And pink. Pink everywhere.

She popped around the corner into the kitchen, while I was left to look over her decorations. One area caught my eye specifically. It was a collection of books on a floating shelf. They were beautifully bound and I paused to read the titles: *Lose Weight like the Loser You Are*. I did a double-take.

Someone had bothered to print that in hard copy and with such a unique binding? *Parts to Steal and Sell out of your Friend's Car without Him Noticing.* That book was bound in black, but no less beautiful. *Ninety-Nine Ways to Please Your Lover with Orange Peels* was placed beside *Things You Can Melt in the Dryer.*

"Shannon, where did you get your books?" I asked, picking up her copy of *The Quitters Guide to Staying out of Jail.*

"What? You mean you never read *A Pyromaniac's Path to Perfection*? Pity. It's an excellent read."

"I have never seen any of these books. No one has ever seen any of these books. Did you manufacture them yourself?"

She scoffed. "I most certainly did not. I enjoy independent writers, and they enjoy me. But I don't loan out my books. I'll never be able to replace them. If you want to read any of them, you have to come here and read them on my sofa." She served me a goblet with a pink bubbling soda inside. "Can you drink this without gagging?"

I turned the cup and examined the bubbles. "Is there something in it I won't like?"

"It's only a problem if you don't like pink."

"Is this a test? Will I shy away from a pink drink because I'm too much of a man to drink pink bubbles?"

She leaned in and whispered, "I have had objections in the past."

"Don't taunt me," I said, before taking a gulp.

She smiled. "What a relief!"

"Are you forgetting that I performed for a ballet on our first date?"

Her laugh was musical. "You'll have to forgive me for jumping you through the usual hoops."

"They're pre-prepared?"

"Well, it's tough for the men when I bring them home and make them feed themselves. They don't exactly know how to do it."

Then I noticed the table she'd set for us. I didn't think it was peculiar when the drinks were served in goblets with stems, but it was peculiar when the salad bowls had stems on them too.

The table was laid with a blush-colored lace table cloth and clear champagne-colored tableware. The silverware was tinted gold.

Bells were playing in the background and suddenly I was filled with a sadness I couldn't ignore.

"Shannon," I said, grasping her elbow and holding her back. "This is all fine. I know you think you're putting yourself and your heart on the line because guys like Simon didn't like this side of you, but this is all fine to me. Whatever you have planned, I'll like it. Stop trembling."

She put her hand on mine. "I know. I'm not shivering because I'm nervous about how you are going to feel about all this. I'm excited because most guys practically have heart attacks looking in from the hallway."

I leaned in and whispered conspiratorially in her ear, "You know what I think this looks like?"

"What?"

"The perfect cover. No one who has ever seen your apartment will ever think that you're a closet vandal." I reached into my pocket. "I have a present for you, but I can tell you for nothing, I would have brought something different if I'd had any idea your place looked like this. I would have got you a necklace that looked like a chandelier. Except the you that I know doesn't wear crystals. She squats in the weeds and writes the word nefelibata in blue spray paint."

"I bet a few people who passed by looked up the definition on their phones," she said.

"I did." I unrolled the wad in my hand. It was a flat shell carved in the shape of a cloud. The iridescent sparkle of mother-of-pearl was little more than a flash in what otherwise was as dull as bone. It had holes drilled into the sides, where delicate brown laces had been attached to make it into a necklace. I pulled it apart between my hands to show her.

Her eyes went wide. "Where did this come from? I've never seen anything like it."

"I made it, little cloud walker. I googled the meaning of your word, and of course, I realized it wasn't just any word you were spray painting on the side of a building. It was a word you chose to describe yourself: a person who walks in the clouds, flouts convention, and lives in a world of their own. It suits you quite well. You're here, and we can all see you, but no one can go on your adventures with you unless you invite them along."

She was a little breathless as she took the shell from me and the light in her eyes caught fire. She wrapped her hand around the back of my neck and pulled me down to kiss her. She pushed me against the fridge. I was about to flip her over, so she was the one pushed against the fridge when a timer on the oven sounded.

She broke away from me and reached for her oven mitts. She hesitated, as she realized she still held the necklace in her hand and she did not want to put it down. To my surprise, she stuffed her whole hand with the necklace in her palm into the oven mitt and opened the oven door.

"Why don't you go have a seat at the table?" she commanded in the form of a question, while she brought out the garlic bread.

In the kitchen, I saw that she had prepared a salad and steaks.

I chuckled.

She was going to make me cut steak on a plate that had a stem. It was the sort of plate that was normally used to serve cake, but I was going to have to cut my steak on it. It would surely wobble everywhere. It must be a very successful practical joke for Shannon to do it as part of her routine when she had a man over for dinner.

"When was the last time you made dinner for a date like this?" I asked her, as she fumbled with the knots in the necklace. "You don't put it on that way," I told her gently.

"How do you put it on?"

"You have to put the whole thing over your head and then pull the strings tight. They'll come loose again when you want to take it off. But you don't need to wear it now. It'll ruin your hair and it doesn't match your dress."

She glared at me. "Do you know how often I'm given presents from men?"

"All the time?"

"Yes! All the time!" she snapped. Then she seemed to realize that admitting to such a thing was a little awkward. She softened. "I don't usually like them. Often I pawn them for 'art' supplies."

Her air quotes made me smile.

"I don't even remember the last time a man gave me a present I wanted to keep."

"Come here. I'll help you get it on."

I helped her and we ate dinner. The thing I noticed the most about Shannon's cooking was that she made food that was the same kind of food as what my mother made, but it did not taste the same. My mother's cooking was filled with butter and cream. Shannon cooked with spices and oil.

Looking at her across the table, she made jokes and ended up feeding me chocolate mousse across a table so tiny that our kneecaps clanked against each other. The neckline of her dress moved with her, and, more than once, I saw more than she intended me to see.

She licked the spoon and said, "I have a little after-dinner game for us to play."

"Afterwards," I said deliberately. "I want to take you to my apartment."

"Why? We've already had dessert."

"It's not to feed you," I said, feeling a little queasy at what I was about to suggest. "I have not done any special cleaning or made any special preparations. I didn't plan to ask you to come to my place tonight. But I want to show you who I am and what I am normally like. Your apartment is very glitzy and before I saw it, I felt that you and I would fit each other nicely. I may

have even been stupid enough to think that your home would
look exactly like mine."

She looked at me with eyes as wide as an owl's.

"You don't want to come?" I asked.

She bit the side of her lip. "We can play a game any night,"
she said as she stood up.

Chapter Fourteen
After Dinner License Plates

Shannon

"You seem spooked that I invited you over," Fletch said to me as we pushed our way through the evening wind.

I hesitated. So far, our relationship had felt like a daydream to me. Like it wasn't real. I had been slowly checking things I'd always wanted to do with a guy I really liked off my list. I'd taken him to the library, defaced various buildings and bus shelters. We'd put up flyers and I'd invited him over to my place for dinner. He had given me something beautiful and meaningful, which was something I couldn't make him do.

My list was getting dangerously short. I wasn't sure if there was that much left for us to do. It was getting to the point where Fletch was going to have to start leading the relationship if he wanted it to keep going. I only had so much inspiration and I couldn't be inspired by a boring man.

And all the men I knew were boring.

It wasn't that Fletch was boring. It was that whenever I let a man lead the relationship it always sucked. They didn't have any fun ideas of things to do. They just wanted to watch the game, watch a movie, watch TV, and watch me.

I didn't know what they found so fascinating about watching me. It wasn't like I threw the same kind of parties for all the men I knew that I threw for Fletch. Most of them barely got to lay a finger on me. Well, I wouldn't have minded if Fletcher put more than his fingers on me, but I was waiting to make that decision.

Apparently, he was taking me to his apartment that he hadn't cleaned. It didn't sound hopeful. Maybe it sounded particularly hopeless after all the work I'd done for our dinner date.

The dress was new. I had shopped for three days to find it. My hairdo took two hours. I had spent a solid hour grooming while I waited for my hair to set. I had taken three bags of old stuff to the Salvation Army to help make my apartment look tidier. Preparing the meal had taken two days and I didn't even want to calculate how long I had been practicing my cooking for just such an occasion.

"Are you spooked?" Fletch asked me, pulling me out of my reverie.

"Aren't you scared?" I replied.

"That you won't like my place?"

"Yeah."

"Shannon, I don't want to have a fake relationship with you. What we've done together so far feels a little fake."

"What do you mean?"

"I mean, tonight you put your best foot forward. I'm thrilled. I had a great time. You look beautiful and everything you fed me tasted amazing. The thing is," he paused. "None of my previous girlfriends have done anything like that for me."

I cocked my head and raised an eyebrow. "What's wrong with them?"

"They didn't see me the way you do. For them, I wasn't the guy they had to work to impress. I was a throwaway guy who they could see as a friend, fool around with when they were lonely, come to for advice when the guy they really wanted wasn't cooperating, and I would soothe them. And Shannon, I am good at soothing a woman. You're not getting the best part of me with your act."

The wind whipped a curl across my face. I looked away and corrected my hair. He sounded like a disappointment. I bit my lips together and felt the downpour of my daydreams fall so deep inside me I could feel them in my ankles. Fletch was going to be the biggest disappointment of my life.

"You always want to be cast that way, do you? You want to be a girl's second-best guy? The nice guy who doesn't get the girl?" I stopped walking. I did not need to be out in all that wind and walk all the way to his place only to walk back again if things couldn't go well. "Fletch, are you trying to turn the tables on me?"

"What do you mean?"

"I mean, are you trying to treat me the way you think I treated Simon? Turn me into a girl who can't really be with you, but who knows where you live and somewhere comfortable to go, but who can never be with you? Now that I'm thinking about it, you've never said anything to make me think we're a couple."

"You told me you always throw out the guys who ask for monogamous relationships," he reminded me patiently.

"Would you have asked for one if I didn't say that?"

His hands were in his pockets, but his gray eyes looked across at me more brilliantly than if his eyes had been made of mirrors. "Well, I'm not seeing anyone else. You don't want a man to control you, so I haven't asked you to reserve yourself only for me. Are you seeing someone else?"

"I'm not."

"Then I guess we're monogamous," he said as his hand sprang from his pocket and took mine. In the next second, he put his arm around me and hurried me down the street. "It's too windy to stay out here. You're going to get an earache."

I was a bit breathless, but he was right, I was going to get an earache if I didn't get out of the wind soon.

"I'll drive you when I take you home."

The door to his apartment was situated on the side of the fragrance shop I liked. He pulled out his key and opened the door. Inside, there was a single staircase going up. My heels clanked on the stairs as he took me up to the top. He opened a second door and led me inside.

My first impression was that his apartment was big. Then I realized it was big because there were no walls. There wasn't even a wall for the bathroom. There was a tub, sink, and a toilet against a wall, but there were no dividers, not even a single thing to indicate the apartment had been zoned.

His bed was in the middle of the room. It was half made, but only because his mattress was the size of my apartment and he was only one man, so he didn't use the whole thing. There was a clothing rack with his clothes on it and he used a cubicle shelf with fabric baskets in it for a dresser.

He walked over to a space heater that had a pair of sweatpants draped over it and picked them up. "Take your shoes off," he said as he made his way back to me.

I kicked off my heels, but I couldn't see why I needed to. The floor was exposed cement and he only had two rugs. One by the tub and another on his side of the bed.

He dropped to his knees and rubbed the warm fabric of the sweatpants against my leg. I was freezing.

"Put these on," he offered.

The heat as I slipped my feet in was unreal on my cold legs as he pulled them up around my waist under my dress.

"You just keep those on the space heater?" I asked, feeling odd.

"I do. It's all part of the nice guy thing. I'm not just nice to women, I'm also nice to myself, and clothes on the heater are a must. At least, until summer." He absently corrected the sheets on his bed, before flopping down on the duvet cover and giving me another smile. "Have a look around. I'll get you some slippers if you like."

"Har har. If I let you, I'm sure you could find clothes to replace everything I'm wearing, and I can wear them as long as you can get me out of what I'm wearing now?"

He smiled brightly. "Look around."

I trod on the hems of Fletch's sweatpants as I wandered around the place. I went over to the kitchen sink. His cupboards had no doors. It wasn't a chic look. It was just old cupboards with no doors. All the dishes he had were ugly. Forget gold-tinted cutlery because nothing matched anything else he owned. Every single piece had been purchased at the Salvation Army and no attempt had been made to make the pieces match. There were brown bowls beside green ones.

The walls were exposed brick, but there were still things on the walls. The most prominent piece was a line of old license plates. "Where did these come from?" I asked, turning back to Fletch.

He had gotten under the covers. "They're from the old cars I've owned."

I glanced back at them. There were fifteen of them. "You've had fifteen cars?"

"I've had more than fifteen. Those are just how many of them had a license plate I could pilfer."

"Why have you had so many cars?"

"I buy cars that are on their deathbeds and I drive them until they die. The car I'm driving now I've had for two months. I've got a good feeling about her. I think she might last another six months."

"Why do that? Don't you need reliable transportation?"

"The car I'm driving now, I paid three hundred and fifty dollars for. The guy selling her just didn't know how to call the wreckers to get her and she still ran. If she runs for the eight months I predict, I will have spent thirty-eight dollars a month on my car payments. When I call the wreckers, they'll pay me fifty bucks."

"That's less than a monthly bus pass!" I gawked.

"Yeah, except I still have to pay for insurance and gas."

I looked at the license plates again. "Interesting hobby. Were any of them fancy? I mean, when they were new?"

"I have had a couple of BMWs and one time I had a Cadillac."

"Are you a good mechanic, then?"

He stroked the side of his face. "I don't really know. If I can figure out what's wrong with it and if the new part isn't too expensive and if it's not too cold out, then I'll try to fix it. Sometimes, it works out. Sometimes, it doesn't."

The stuff in the corner looked like a hoarder's paradise from a distance, but as I closed in, I realized it was much more. There were wood pieces stacked on power tools and boxes with weird designs carved in the lids. When I tried to open one, I realized it was nailed shut.

"What is this supposed to be?"

"It's a xylophone," he said, biting the side of his thumb and looking at me curiously from under the wings of his eyebrows.

"You make them?"

"Yeah. I sell them on Etsy and eBay."

"Will you play it for me?"

"Sure," he said, throwing the bedclothes aside and lifting himself from the mattress. "But only if you get in the bed."

"I have to get in the bed?" I asked cautiously.

"I've been warming it up for you," he said, stepping past me and pulling a pair of mallets off the wall.

With him on the other side of the room, I approached the bed. There was no couch anywhere in the apartment. There was room for one. There just wasn't one. So, unless I wanted to sit at a chair on the other side of the apartment, I had to climb into his bed.

I felt nervous. If I got into that bed, I was going to smell things. I was going to smell his sweat, aftershave, deodorant, detergent, and anything else. If he ate chips in bed, there might be crumbs.

Across the room, he was setting things up and moving things around. I was being stupid. He was a professional musician. I was being all fidgety for nothing. Besides, didn't I like Fletch more than any other man I had ever dated? The sheets were losing their heat by the second.

I got in.

It was warm, just like he promised. When I took my first breath in, the scent was good. It was clean and slightly tangy, exactly the way the best men smelled. I propped myself up on the pillows and looked around the room. Fletch was not quite done setting up as he lined up xylophone boxes.

The first thing I realized lying there was that I couldn't see a TV. Yes, I slept in an oversized closet, and sometimes I put the TV over the fake mantle when I was expecting a visitor, but most of the time, it was mounted on the wall in my little closet.

"Where's your TV?" I asked.

"I have a tablet I watch stuff on if I must," he replied, lifting a mallet. "This sound works better when I'm part of an orchestra or a band, but all the same... Ready?"

I nodded and he began to play.

It was hard to have an objection to such soft music, like the way rain should sound on the roof, but it never sounds the way it should. It was peaceful. I found myself thinking of meditation exercises I'd done when I used to go to yoga. I started breathing the way I used to breathe when I did my stretches. I found myself thinking of the red balloon and the spot of light. I aligned my spine and eased myself flat on my back. The bed got warmer. The music got softer.

When I woke up, it was the middle of the night and Fletch was asleep beside me. I had slept for hours. I sat up and pushed the covers aside.

His hand came out and caught my wrist. "You don't have plans for tomorrow morning, do you?"

"No. Tomorrow is Saturday."

"Then lay down. Kiss me and relax," he said with his eyes closed.

"Aren't you going to ask for your pants back?"

"I told you to kiss me," his voice cut across the darkness. "I did not ask for more. I won a big battle today, and I want the spoils, but I did not win this war."

"What are you talking about?" I asked, settling next to him.

"We're a couple now, aren't we?"

"Yes."

"You were never going to agree to that. As far as I knew, you were going to be a woman I was seeing who could be seeing someone else on any night that you weren't with me. It was maddening, and now that's over. You're my girlfriend and I can count on you not to date anyone else?"

"Yeah."

"So, give me a goodnight kiss, the same one you'd give me if we were saying goodbye on your doorstep, and go to sleep."

He leaned over me and when his lips touched mine, something inside me broke. It completely broke. Was it his warmth? Was it the way he kissed me? Like I was infinitely precious? Like I was his? Was it the way he tasted or the way he smelled? Was it his bed? Was it the way his voice sounded in the dark?

All I knew as he ended the kiss and settled next to me was that I didn't want to go back to my apartment. I never wanted to go back to my apartment. I wanted to live here, where my feet were warm and where the man next to me was everything I wanted.

I put my hand over my heart. It was pounding.

I had to chill out. He hadn't done the thing I needed him to do. I needed him to show me his idea of a good time and, consequently, of a good life. I had to calm down and let him show me more of who he was. I was just filling in the blanks he felt open with the hot excitement I felt.

I had just worked myself into a feeling of indifferent stupor when he said, his voice clipped and clear in the night air, "I won't look if you want to take off your bra." He turned on his side away from me.

For a second, I was stunned he had spoken to me like that. Then I realized how much it had been digging into my ribs. "Had a lot of girls up here before?" I asked unclipping the back.

"A few. I told you, I have friends who are women. They come for the backrubs and leave me for the wall slams of another man."

"I don't get it. You've slammed me against lots of walls," I said with a chuckle as I pulled my bra out from my sleeve.

"I know. I thought I was the nice guy and she was leaving me for the domineering jerk who slammed her against walls. I was wrong. I was the nice guy who didn't want her... or any of them. If I wanted them as much as I want you, I would have slammed them up against some walls. I wouldn't have been able to let them go to another man. As it was, I could let them leave. I felt a bit sorry, but getting over the letdown was easier than anyone watching could have supposed."

"Well," I said, putting my nose in the air. "I didn't get a backrub."

"That's because if I place one hand on you, things will get out of control. It's our first sleepover. I want you to be comfortable. I want you to stay forever."

And his voice, like liquid darkness, undid me.

Chapter Fifteen
Diamond Smile

Shannon

I woke up on Saturday morning in Fletch's bed. He was cooking at the stove with the sunlight from a skylight turning his hair from auburn to flame. His cooking smelled good.

"Good morning," he said, humming as he flipped over what was in the pan. He favored me with a smile that turned me into a puddle of goo.

"You look happy," I commented as I searched for my bra on the floor by the bed.

"Yeah, well, there are few sights more satisfying than seeing you wake up in my bed."

"Yet, you didn't stay in bed with me."

He chuckled. "I couldn't. My phone has no alarm on it on a Saturday morning."

"Mine doesn't either."

"Are you sure?" he asked, his teeth cutting diamonds out of the morning light. "Cause your phone made about a hundred sounds."

"What time is it?" I asked as I reached for my phone.

"Ten."

He was right. I had fallen asleep early and slept late. It was all because I had woken up in the middle of the night with a million thoughts, worries, the pounding of my heart, and Fletch's irresistible conversation. When I finally did fall asleep, why had I slept so deeply? On a normal day, I got up at seven-thirty and on the weekends, I got up at the same time whether I liked it or not. Why had I slept like a dead person?

I looked around at the bed and everything around me. The answer was everywhere.

I had finally been able to relax. I never relaxed. Tension was the most common thing I experienced on a date. I was always so worried about everything. Thoughts rammed through my brain like express trains passing through a train station. What if I did something stupid? What if I did something I'd regret? What if something happened that I couldn't undo? What if I got hurt?

Across the apartment, Fletch was pulling toast from a toaster and buttering it. "Do you like marmalade?" he asked.

"Yeah. How did you know?"

"*Ninety-Nine Ways to Please Your Lover with Orange Peels*. I assume they must have an entire section on marmalade."

"They do, and an entire section on how to peel an orange in various romantic and sexual ways."

He chuckled and brought my plate over to me. "How do you peel an orange in a sexual way?"

"Well, when kids peel the orange and get the whole peel off in one piece and they say it looks like an elephant with two big ears and a trunk. Adults say--"

He covered his face with his free hand and nodded. "Yeah. Yeah. I get it."

He handed me my plate. It was an omelet with onions, mushrooms, red peppers, and cheese with a piece of marmalade toast on the side.

"I love it. Thank you."

He looked at me. "You should check your phone. There were a lot of text bings."

I glanced at it. "They're messages from my sisters. I'm supposed to be going shopping with them in two hours and I haven't confirmed, so they're getting antsy and asking me how our date went last night."

"What are you going to tell them?"

"That you didn't think my dress was very pretty and replaced it with sweats."

He reached for my phone. "Don't tell them that."

I pulled it away from him. "One of them is single," I explained.

"What's that supposed to mean?"

"Listen to me. I am the type of woman who put a fake gun to a stranger's back and told him he had to come with me--"

He interrupted. "I know. I was there."

"Yes, but what do you think makes a person able to just do that on a whim?"

Leaning on his elbow at the end of the bed, he munched toast triangles. "Practice?"

"Exactly."

He almost choked on his toast. "How many times have you done that?"

"Okay. I hadn't done that particular thing before, but my family is into pranks, jests, tricks, sarcasm, stories that don't go anywhere, and saying the most outrageous thing a person can think of just to get a reaction." I took a breath in. "I stopped bringing my dates home after the eleventh grade. My date never wanted to see me again because my older sister put her tongue in his ear just to watch him jump. I've never seen anyone jump so high. He was sixteen years old and an only child."

"Okay," Fletch said, rolling his tongue around the front of his perfect teeth. "Let's say a person can rise to the challenge of suddenly having a tongue in their ear. What is the correct reaction to that?"

I smacked his knee. "There is no correct reaction to that. That's why she did it. It's undefeatable, though it was utterly misplaced on him. If she had looked straight into his eyes and said, 'You're cute,' she would have undone him. Seriously, if you let her continue to lick your ear without giving her the reaction she craves, it'll become like a staring contest. She'll just keep on licking your ear until you crush your ear into your shoulder. She'd never quit. It's not a fair situation."

"And if a person licks her ear?"

I shook my head and stuck out my tongue. "She knows you want a reaction and she'll give you one, but she'd make you sorry by saying the worst thing that pops into her head. She'd yowl that you'd licked her brain and you might not be able to keep it together. And there's not one of them who wouldn't get involved once they started. My married sister-in-law would join in as well as my mother and my grandmother.."

"So… if this is a game your whole family plays, why are you telling me the backdoor? And why did you tell them you had a date?"

"I didn't tell them I had a date. My sisters like to go shopping together. We go almost every weekend, and one of them realized I was shopping for a dress. Then she made up a story that I was buying a dress to wear on a date, which I denied emphatically, but it wasn't good enough."

"Because they saw our pictures on social media?"

I frowned deeply. "Yes. I have put up lots of pictures with guys before, but I don't usually get a lot of notice from my family because they know the guys I see are tissue paper… I'm not going to keep using them. Except, when they got the idea that I had a date I was buying a dress for, they looked up my feed and found the picture of us making out against the side of the wall."

Fletch smiled broadly.

"Funny. I didn't think you liked that picture."

He continued smiling. "The content of the picture is not what I'm enjoying at the moment. I'm just interested in the backlash you experienced. When I had to explain that photo to my mother, I thought I was alone. I had no idea your family would come after you for it. What did they think?"

"They thought it was a prank," I admitted.

"Wait. Wait. Wait," Fletch said, sitting up all the way. "You're telling me this because you're thinking of introducing me to your family?"

"It's not so much that I'm thinking of introducing you to them as acknowledging that I might not be able to protect you from them everlastingly." I filled my mouth with omelet and waited for Fletch to answer.

He nodded. "Sounds fun."

"It won't be," I assured him.

Chapter Sixteen
A Wrong Phone Number is a Rejection

Shannon

On Monday morning, I was back at the office and there was a commotion coming from the back offices. Peeking around the corner, I saw Natalie's yellow hair bob up and down from inside Levi's office.

I took off my coat, put my lunch in the fridge and went to my desk, where I turned on my computer.

I tried not to be concerned or interested in whatever was going on with Natalie. People who hit me over the head with bricks were none of my business. I listened to the office voicemail and returned a couple of calls. I checked my email and composed a few responses.

It was past nine o'clock when Levi's door opened and Natalie came bouncing into the hallway. Whatever had happened, it was in her favor. Keeping my interest to a minimum, I did not see who else had been in the meeting until they had meandered all the way to the front desk.

I glanced up to see the dark hair and striking features of Carver Criche. He was smiling, but it wasn't the same smile or excitement I had seen on his face the day he kidnapped me with a cookie. It was his work face, a studied smile as part of a permanently interested expression.

"Thank you, again," Natalie was saying to him. "Being able to go on tour with a DJ like Falconhands is a huge honor."

"It's a training ground," he said optimistically. "If you do it well, who knows where it will take you?"

Natalie squared her shoulders and gave him a confident grin.

I put my pen in my mouth like I was smoking a cigarette and inhaled. It was the only way to watch the events unfolding in front of me and keep my composure. He'd given her a contract? DJ Falconhands was a rising star who used a different soloist for almost every track on an album. When he toured, he took all the soloists with him. Someone must have dropped out and Natalie was going to cover their position. It was the chance of a lifetime, but the position was also precarious, and easy to blow. I wondered if a woman who hit people over the head with bricks could hold that kind of place without blowing it.

It would certainly be interesting to watch.

Then I looked at Carver. I had to look at him. He was staring at me. The last time I saw him I had given him that fake phone number. From his expression, he was finished with Natalie and Levi. He wanted them out of the room so he could have a moment with me.

What could be contained in that moment? I couldn't guess. The only thing I hoped was that he had arranged for Natalie to have that job because her singing was good enough for her to have earned it. The worst thing I could think of, while she prattled her thanks to him, was that he had given it to her because he knew that would be a seamless way for him to see me again without arousing suspicion and to pump her for information. It wasn't a completely far-fetched thought. Men had done crazy things for me before when they thought they were losing their chance with me. He probably didn't know she was the one who made those posters of him and only remembered her from the night we were supposed to kidnap him.

As Natalie talked, he gave her cursory glances, tearing his eyes away from mine whenever the conversation demanded it.

I stared back at him daring him to make his next move. How was he going to get rid of Natalie and Levi?

I had to admit, I was surprised by the resolution.

"Natalie, don't you have a million things to do to prepare?" Levi suddenly cut in. "You said you were going to get your blonde touched up and if you're going to fly to Toronto tonight, then hadn't you better get going?"

"Ah, yes," she said, but her eyes fixed on Carver with the same intensity his eyes fixed on me. She was completely starstruck by him and didn't want to leave his side. After all, he was not going on tour with her. His part in her becoming a star was complete… for the time being. "I'm just so thankful for this opportunity," she continued as she inched toward the door.

"Shannon," Levi said, taking a step toward me. "Carver is going to book three solo recording sessions for Jeremy Stevens from Stark Mad. Work him into the schedule, would you?"

Natalie left the building at the same time Levi disappeared back down the hall.

Carver and I were alone.

Averting my eyes, I sat back in my chair and pulled up our booking app. "What times did you have in mind, Mr. Criche?"

He covered the space between us like a jungle cat stalking its prey, which was hilarious because we were in a well-lit office before noon, but men who lived in clubs couldn't really walk any other way. He leaned against the high edge of my desk like he was leaning against a bar about to order drinks.

"We don't have vodka or soda," I said playfully before I could hold it back. I bit my tongue with my side molars. I was going to have to learn to rein myself in if I wanted to date Fletch exclusively.

"The number you gave me the other night. It didn't make sense," he said.

It was the one I had printed on dozens of posters. "What didn't make sense?"

"Why did you and Natalie want to kidnap me?"

"You could have asked her. She was just here," I deflected.

He smiled. "I did. She said it was because you had a thing for me. She said you'd seen me numerous times because of your work and you wanted to meet me. She said she was doing what you asked her to do when she hit you over the head with the brick and handcuffed you to that guy in the camp kitchen. She said you weren't even hurt. It was all part of your plot to meet me."

Whatever Natalie did in the future, nothing would surprise me. She had turned that story upside down, blamed everything on me, and let herself off the hook for assault. What did it matter to her? She was flying out to join DJ Falconhands' tour.

I smiled patiently. "I'm afraid that is a bit of a distortion. I'm sorry your name somehow got mixed up in our games, but…"

He leaned further in and interrupted me. "I want to get mixed up in your games."

I continued speaking like he hadn't said anything, "But if what Natalie told you was true, then why didn't I give you my real number when I had the chance?"

"That's why this doesn't make sense," he said smoothly.

"Well, whatever was going on that night, the situation has changed."

"How?"

"Well, that guy I was handcuffed to in the camp kitchen?"

"What about him?"

"I ended up really liking him. I liked him so much I'm dating him exclusively now, so can I book you those times for Jeremy Stevens?" I said, trying to end on a professional note.

When I looked back to Carver for an answer, he was removing a pair of sunglasses from the case and placing them on his face like his job was to preserve the lost art of being cool. "I'm not sure when Jeremy can fit a recording session into his schedule. I'll have to get my assistant to call you with his availability." With that, he swept from the building.

I was glad he was gone, but Levi wouldn't like that Carver had put off booking. I bet his assistant never called. I bet the whole thing was a lame ploy so he could talk to me and if I was in a relationship then none of it was worth it to him.

I went back to doing my regular work.

Chapter Seventeen
Rock Candy Girl

Fletch

"Hey Chester," I said as I walked between the deserted tables of the Eloquent Spider. I'd never been to the club when it was still light out, or seen the place so empty. Even a twenty-eight-year-old songstress singing Sarahific covers brought in more people than just one person at a table. It was a club that hosted up-and-coming bands, so I'd played there many times. I played, but I didn't hang out. There was something in the air I didn't like. Some people thought the atmosphere was exciting, but I thought it was frenzied. Everyone at the Eloquent Spider wanted something too much.

The old friend of mine wasn't much different.

"I'm only tolerating you calling me Chester because we've known each other since we were nine, but if you call me anything but Chase in front of another human…"

"I know. I don't need my vocal cords to play the drums," I said with a smile as I took a seat across from my old buddy.

Chase and I had been grubby little boys together, been in many different bands together as teens, and eventually, he chose the club scene and I chose the orchestra. Neither of them paid well. For me, it wasn't about the pay. It was about beauty, so even though I played the drummer for him whenever I could, our worlds had mostly split. He was the one who set me up to play for City of Vines the night Shannon kidnapped me.

Now he sat across from me. His hair was cut well, albeit, poorly styled. He wore olive sunglasses over his eyes and a black leather jacket, showing the tattoos on his fingers, and the metal bracelets on his wrists. He didn't play or sing anymore, but floated through the industry, hooking this person up with that person. He'd been the manager of the Eloquent Spider for two years. I liked how the job grounded him, but I still didn't have the heart to hang out in his club on a Saturday night if I wasn't going to play.

"You were so secretive over the phone," I said. "Why didn't you want to tell me who you are planning to introduce me to? I'm not likely to turn into a fanboy and scream it from the rooftops, even if you are introducing me to someone good."

"Fletch, that's the most annoying thing about you. You never get excited. It's like the music doesn't get under your skin the way it does for other people. Do you ever get songs stuck in your head?"

I shrugged.

He had a case. We were friends, but we were very different. Chase had a wall of pictures in his office of selfies with him and musical celebrities. I could usually recognize them, but he also just liked to get his picture taken with the most beautiful women who came into the club. Sometimes, they were famous, sometimes not. They sure prettied up his wall, and it made him look like he'd accomplished something I couldn't, even though I had a master's degree.

"I dunno. Music sounds like math to me," I agreed.

"Well, I'm introducing you to the lead singer of Blades and Blasters. Her name is Ringlet and she may very well be the most desirable woman on earth. Beautiful, talented, smart, she checks everyone's boxes."

For Chase to say that, she must be something special, but she couldn't be prettier than Shannon. I scoffed, "You make it sound like you're setting us up on a date instead of a gig. Aren't I just supposed to drum for her?"

He regarded me levelly. "She asked for you specifically."

"Oh?"

"Yeah. Her drummer sprained his wrist and she wants to give him a week off, so she asked me if I could get you to play for their Friday and Saturday night shows while they're in town. Asked for you, using your full name, no hesitation. I wondered if you already knew her."

"How would I know her? Did she previously moonlight as a violinist?"

"I don't know where she heard your name, but she clicked her ravishing tongue and had this sick little grin on her face like meeting you would be the highlight of her tour stop. What the hell?"

"Unless Ringlet is not her real name, then I have no idea who she is or what's going through her head, Chester."

He pointed a tattooed finger at me. "Don't call me that. Seriously."

"Fine. Where is she?"

"She should be down any minute. I told her you'd be here at one."

I rolled my tongue around my mouth and looked at the clock on the wall. It was a few minutes after one.

Chase drummed his fingers on the table. "She's using my office to make a call."

"Oh, that's why we're down here? She couldn't use her dressing room?"

"She says it isn't soundproof. I always thought it was," Chase said, casting his eyes across the ceiling. His office was directly above the spot he stared at. He leaned back in his chair. "Anything new with you?"

"I have a new girlfriend," I said as nonchalantly as I could manage.

Immediately, Chase's face lit up. As soon as I was tied up with a woman and not in competition for Ringlet's affection, everything was fine. "Why didn't you say so?"

"I am saying so."

"What's her name?"

"Shannon Bilx."

"Shit. Isn't that Simon's old girlfriend? What are you doing with her?"

I shook my head slowly. "He's known I was seeing her, but it's pretty new that we decided to knot ourselves off for some more exclusive time together."

"He must be pissed."

"Yeah. He is, but…" I chuckled. "I can't bring myself to care. She's amazing. All wrong for Simon and all right for me." I was talking too much. I shut my mouth and stroked the stubble on my chin.

Chase was nodding appreciatively. "From what he told me, she's a huge player. What makes you think she's not playing with you?"

"I think she's the type of woman who would always make you feel like she was playing you because she is. I don't think she can turn that off. She's so playful. From what she says, she comes from a long line of prankers, tricksters, and people who don't know when to stop."

"And you're okay with that? Don't you eventually want to be with a grown-up woman and not just a fun lay?"

I resented him referring to her like that, but I also knew it was only concern for me and the aftereffect of having seen the figurative hole she'd left in Simon's chest.

"I don't know if I've thought of it that way. If I could say one thing about it, I'd say that Simon chased her. I haven't done that. She's come after me."

"Is her pool of admirers running dry?"

"I doubt it."

"Have you got a picture? I don't think I ever met her personally when she was with Simon."

"I hadn't either."

Chase took out his phone and got on social media. Within seconds, he'd found the picture of us making out against the wall. His face lit up. "That could be an album cover. Well, I hope she's not jerking you around, my friend."

"And I hope night doesn't fall before your girl comes downstairs."

"I'll ask Renee to see what's keeping her." He dialed his office number to get the phone on his assistant's desk, but just as Renee picked up, Ringlet came around the corner.

I didn't recognize her. Her head was shaved up one side and dyed the most vibrant color of neon purple a person could think of. Up close, her face was like a porcelain doll or like a painted mask. There were so few lines and so little movement, I wondered if she'd had work done, and how she could have made the expression Chase described when she asked for me. Didn't she have so much filler and botox in her face that she couldn't move it now if she wanted to?

"Hey," she said drolly as she approached. "How's it going?"

"Ringlet, this is Fletch, the drummer you asked for."

"So, it's you?" I was wrong about her face, as soon as she realized who I was, her face came alive, bending in lines that made her interest as obvious as the look on her face.

I stood up and put out my hand. She took my hand in hers and jerked me toward her. Our faces were closer together than was comfortable for me and I tried to shake her loose, but she held on tightly. "You're cute," she said before she let me go.

She pulled out a chair and sat down between Chase and me. Turning her chair completely toward me she started, "So, we want you for rehearsal tomorrow and again before the show on Friday. From what I've heard about you, you should have no trouble keeping up, but still, I want to make sure you know the songs and nothing surprises you. I don't have a stylist for my band. I dress all my boys myself. Take off your shirt."

I glanced at Chase, who was so green with envy that the rest of his face matched his sunglasses.

Then I looked again at Ringlet. Her eyes were blue and almost as luminescent as a droid's. I tried to figure out what was so special about her, but I came up at a loss. She had a fine body and had dressed it well, but I realized immediately that I was not getting the same kind of treatment Chase had received.

The way she treated him was probably the way she treated everyone to get the results she wanted. It was a skilled kind of manipulation intended to make her object feel special, but also to keep them at arm's length. I saw it all the time among musicians. For some reason, I was excluded from that performance. What I thought probably didn't matter, because she was coming on so strong, it almost gave me whiplash.

All the same, what she wanted was not ridiculous if she was going to dress me. I had been fitted for many pieces in my many years as a performer, and I had been compelled to change my clothes in many strange places. It was fine. I could do what she asked without squealing.

I stood up and removed my coat. I was wearing a button-up-the-front shirt with a white undershirt underneath. I started with the buttons at the bottom of my shirt to make myself feel less like a stripper, but I didn't miss the hungry way Ringlet observed me. I folded it before setting it in a square bundle on the table. Then, with one hand, I grabbed the back of the collar of the white undershirt and pulled it over my head in one motion.

I stood, staring at her, and held my shirt in one hand.

"Nice six-pack," she commented as her eyes searched my skin. "That's a lot of freckles, dude."

"I have red hair," I replied without interest.

"The freckles go all the way down," Chase commented before he could stop himself. The man had known me since I was nine.

"You know that, do you?" she said, clicking her tongue.

Chase scrambled with an explanation about our relationship Ringlet wasn't interested in, while she got up and walked around me, inspecting me.

Finally, she said, "I like your freckles. They make you look different. Why don't you have any tattoos?"

"I do. You just can't see them."

"Oh?" she clucked, raking her eyes across my lower body.

I didn't flinch, but answered, "They're in the chambers of my heart."

In response, a look crossed her features. It was a look that was half excitement, half desire, and I realized with sudden clarity that Shannon almost always had that look on her face when she was with me.

Ringlet took two solid breaths to steady herself before she said, "Call me Rin. All my best friends call me Rin."

I nodded.

She came closer and touched the undershirt I held clutched in my hand like she wanted to touch me, but knew she shouldn't. "You know, I wasn't planning on making you over. I was just going to pick up a few togs like what our normal drummer wears and put them on you, but I've changed my mind. I want you to perform with your shirt off. I'll cut your hair, buy you boots, trousers, and I'll find something for you to wear around your neck."

"My hair is fine. I don't need a cut."

"You do," she said in a way that couldn't be argued with. "The way you look right now, you're a nine. That's good. It gives me a lot to work with, but we're rock stars, and I need you to be an eleven. Come upstairs. I'll cut your hair in my dressing room." She licked her lips. "You're going to make me famous."

"You're not going to use my office?" Chase cut in.

"I don't need it anymore," she called as she led the way to the back stairs.

I pulled my shirt apart to see its shape so I could put it back on when Chase came around the table to hiss in my face, "What are you, a stripper? How can you take your clothes off like that in front of a woman?"

"I didn't think it was that provocative," I hedged.

"What the hell? Don't you have a girlfriend? And when did you learn to say crap like that to a woman? You got her looking at your junk and then thinking about your heart? Who are you? You could have nailed her on the table if I hadn't been here."

I had no interest in sleeping with Ringlet. But Chase was right. Where had that come from? "I don't know. Shannon talks like that."

"Can I use that line?" he asked, as perplexed as he was annoyed.

I shrugged my shoulders. "If you can line it up."

Chase practically spat in vexation as he followed Ringlet up the stairs.

Chapter Eighteen
Plug her Ears so She Keeps her Eyes Open

Shannon

I stood on the street waiting for Fletch. He told me to put on something fun and meet him at the bus stop on Agate Street. It was right next to the Eloquent Spider and there was a lineup of people waiting to get in. I breathed a sigh of relief that he wasn't going to make me go in there. I worked in the music industry. I didn't need to go to a club to hear the music up close.

I texted him when I got there and he texted back to say that he was on his way, but it had been five minutes and a few guys from the lineup had started to take an interest in me. I eyed them wearily. I was so over their type.

When Fletch arrived, it was like he ran in from out of nowhere. He looked different. For one thing, he was wearing a white shirt with none of the buttons done up. His hair had been cut and he hadn't shaved, so his chin looked scratchy in a stylish way. He had a black triangle inked on the side of his neck and a silver cuff on his ear. Returning my eyes to his hair, someone had done a top-notch job cutting it. I always knew Fletch was attractive, but before his look had been soft. He looked like the type of man you could cuddle up with. The new haircut gave him a completely different look. Now, the only word I could think of to describe him was cut. I hadn't even known the muscles of his stomach looked like that.

I looked at him, shy and confused. "What happened to you?"

"Rin," he said, reaching into the front pocket of his black leather pants. At first, I thought he'd taken out a condom and I was about to smack him when he put the package to his white teeth and tore at the side. The plastic was clear and he was opening a pair of earplugs. "I'm playing with Blades and Blasters tonight. I thought you might like to come if you didn't have to cart a drum kit. We played last night and everyone loved us, so I decided to invite you tonight. But I'm not risking your sensitive ears, so I got you these. If you don't have a good time, feel free to leave. It won't break my heart, but as this is the last night I'm playing with them, I thought I'd invite you anyway. It's kind of a once-in-a-lifetime chance. Can you put them in yourself?"

I shook my head, though it was a lie. I had worn earplugs more times than I could count, but I loved the idea of him taking care of me, so I watched him roll them between his fingers and slide each one into position. They were warm. They'd been in his pants.

"You look beautiful," he said.

"I can hear you, if that's what you're wondering," I said, trying to keep my excitement in check.

"Great. I'll get you through the ticket gate." He took my hand and got it stamped.

Inside, the opening band was playing, and Fletch turned me in his arms. He twirled me and pulled me against his bare chest. I wanted to ask him if he had always been the man who appeared in front of me, but a quiet question was impossible. Instead, I watched him as he danced and pulled me along with him. I moved my feet and wondered if I had just somehow missed seeing him because I was so caught up in my own act. Was I so focused on making sure that I came off right that I had missed that I was with a man who was sexy, confident, and exciting?

At that exact moment, someone tapped him on the shoulder and indicated the stage. It was time for him to go. He nodded, slipped his arm around me, and kissed the side of my head before he disappeared into the crowd.

With him gone, I was a little breathless and a little unsure of what to do with myself. It wasn't like I knew anyone there. I looked around before deciding that I needed to get a view of the stage or I wouldn't see Fletch performing. That had been one thing about the ballet. Everyone was well organized in their seats, so it was easy to see him in his tux.

However, once the opening band left the stage, everyone crowded toward the platform and I was swept aside.

Suddenly, I felt someone grab my upper arm. I turned to see Carver staring back at me. "If you can't see, I can take you upstairs," he called loudly over the din of the crowd.

I wouldn't have gone with him, but I saw Renee at his elbow. Renee and I were business contacts and I'd spoken to her many times. She was clearly with Carver, so I nodded and went up the backstairs to a viewing room that had wide plate glass to watch the show from above without the ruckus of the club below.

Inside, Renee introduced me to Chase, the owner of the club. With one look at him, I could tell that the club scene was his whole life.

"So, you're Fletch's girl?" he said with an unpleasant smack of his lips like he was dressing me down.

I looked at him sideways.

He straightened and corrected himself. "Fletch told me he was inviting you tonight, but I didn't know which one you were, so Carver and Renee pointed you out for me. Fletch and I are old friends."

"Pleasure to meet you," I said indifferently. "Is it really okay for me to watch the show from up here?"

"Absolutely," Chase said.

I thanked him and moved over to Renee, who was right up against the glass watching.

She whispered something to me, but I couldn't hear her, so I pulled out an earplug. "Come again?"

"Are you really dating him?" she asked, pointing to Fletch, who had just come out onto the stage completely shirtless.

My heart caught on the sight of him and almost stopped. The other band members were moving around, taking their positions, but the drum set was lit by a spotlight and he was the only thing anyone could see. He took up the drum sticks and it felt like the show started with him. The rest of the stage lit up, showing two guitarists and the singer, but who was interested in them?

"Yeah," I muttered to Renee. "He's my boyfriend."

"You need to watch out for Ringlet," she warned. "She wants him so bad, it's coming out of her ears."

"She's the singer? Isn't he only playing with them tonight? How can it matter what she thinks of him after tomorrow when she moves onto her next tour destination?"

Renee rolled her eyes. "This warning isn't for next week. It's for tonight. It's timely! Do not let that man out of your sight."

I leaned against the wall. "He won't cheat on me."

Renee shrugged. "If you say so."

Chase's phone rang and after exchanging a few brief words with the person on the other end of the line, he stood up. "Renee, we've got a problem. Come back to the office with me. Please excuse us. We'll be right back."

As soon as they were gone, I again felt Carver's eyes boring into me. Was he checking out my butt or killing me with the daggers in his eyes? I wasn't overly curious, but my self-preservation instincts made me turn to evaluate the threat.

When I saw his expression, I was a bit taken aback. He was looking at me like the act of looking at me satisfied him. Which was weird. No one just wanted to look at me. Everyone wanted to touch. "What do you want?" I asked smoothly.

"Do you know, I never feel envious."

"Really?"

"Yeah. I have never wanted something someone else has. I only want what I have or what I can get for myself. What other people have is none of my concern. Except, I do feel… what would you call it… rage when someone takes something that doesn't belong to them."

"Hmmm. What has been taken from you?"

"You."

"How so?"

"You were supposed to put that gun into my back," he said, fire in his voice.

"It wasn't a real gun," I said, with water in my tone.

He scoffed and took a step closer to me. "There was more going on that night than you are admitting. You or Natalie is lying to me. But why?"

I put up my hand to stop him from saying anything more. "Listen, none of that old stuff matters. I am no longer friends with Natalie and you gave her the chance of a lifetime signing her up with DJ Falconhands even though you know she's violent. You saw her behave violently. I left that night with Fletch and he was so good to me, I never want to leave him, no matter how much or how little he has."

"But if you had kidnapped me as you planned, I would have been the one you left with?"

"Ah. You feel cheated," I acknowledged.

"You called him by my name, drove the barrel of a gun into his back, and made him go with you," he explained with exasperation.

I regarded him curiously. "And you've always wanted a woman to do that to you?"

"I haven't wanted just any woman to do that. I didn't even know who you were, but the moment I saw you, I knew I was being cheated. It should have been me."

I cocked my head to the side. "But, it wasn't."

"Listen, I did the cookie thing and asked for your number. You gave me that ridiculous slip of paper and I fell for it. I came to your office, I tried to make it clear that I want a date with you, and you shut me down saying you're seeing this guy," he whined, waving a hand at Fletch through the glass. "I just want one date with you. I'm sure I can put everything back to the way it is supposed to be if you'll give me a few hours."

"Carver, I don't think you understand. Fletch did something to me," I said conspiratorially.

Wide-eyed, he asked, "What?"

"He made me fall in love with him, and I fell… hard."

"Oh? You like this little show? You must know that I am a producer for Blades and Blasters. Rin is one of my stars and I told her to ask Chase for Fletch to play at this show. Do you think he'd rather go on tour with her or stay here and date you?"

I looked down at the stage. He was twirling the drumstick he wasn't using in his free hand. From his expression, his smile, and the way he thumped out the rhythm of the song, it looked like one of life's highs. He had not looked like that when he played the triangle for the orchestra.

Carver came up behind me. "One's fortune and fame, with a famous beauty at his side. And the other is what? What do you have to offer him, Shannon?"

What Carver wasn't saying was that if Fletch turned down the offer, and Shannon didn't come to Carver on her own, he would do everything he could to make sure that Fletch never got a decent job again.

Whatever Fletch thought of the deal, I had to handle things in my own way, so I turned to Carver and answered, "The barrel of a gun between the third and fourth ribs. I've heard that's pretty desirable."

"One date," Carver continued. "Is all I'm asking for."

I was tired of talking to him. He was boring and he was ruining the pleasure of watching Fletch. I sighed and pretended to relent. "Listen, even if you are only asking for one date, I think you want something rather specific. Why don't you make me a list, describing your fantasy date in as much detail as possible and I'll see what I can do for you?"

Color flooded his cheeks. "Do you want it by tonight?"

I leaned toward the band playing. "There's no need to rush. It's your perfect date. You don't want to be too hasty. Take your time and really think about what you want." I put my earplug back in and hoped that was enough to signal the end of our conversation.

Chapter Nineteen
Overripe

Shannon

I got Carver's email on Monday delivered to my work email, which was less than ideal. I forwarded it to my personal email and deleted it from the work computer. At lunch, I huddled under my desk and read his wish list.

He wanted me to surprise him and lead him away at gunpoint. He also wanted to be handcuffed the whole way, both hands.

Once we were at what he called 'the first location', he wanted me to eat something with a tantalizing aroma and refuse to share it with him.

He wanted me to undo a few buttons on his shirt and run the barrel of a gun along his bare skin.

After that, it got pretty fuzzy, as he wanted me to make up the rest. Mostly what he wanted was whatever happened with Fletch. He didn't know that Fletch had paid Natalie so he could scold me.

I met Fletch for dinner at a deli between our two apartments. Fletch's new look caused a stir wherever he went, but at least three women were staring at him across the dining room as if they'd never seen a man before.

"I ordered a sandwich for you," he said after he greeted me with a kiss.

"Has it got mustard and olives on it?"

He smiled. "Yes."

"Good. You have my permission to order for me anytime you feel so inclined." I stumbled over to a table and he followed me.

"You haven't got your usual bag with you. Are we not going out tonight?"

He was referring to my bag of spray paint, which I had not remembered to pick up. I stuck out my tongue. "Tonight, we have to talk about Carver Criche. Do you remember him?"

"Only from the dog molestation posters."

I snorted. "My brain has done a complete about-face on that issue. We should put those posters back up."

"Why?"

"Because he's been harassing me."

Fletch stared at me like he couldn't believe his eyes when the lady at the counter called him to pick up his order. He came back with sandwiches, chips, and fountain drinks. "Sorry? He's been doing what?"

I told Fletch about the cookie handcuffs, the visit to my office, him sending Natalie away, Fletch's gig, and how Carver had been behind it, and finally, I showed him the list of things he wanted on his date with me.

Fletch read the list with an ashen face. "Does he think you're going to do all this?"

"I implied I might, just to get him to back off."

"Should we do it?"

I almost choked on my pop. "Should we do what?"

"Should we take him on the date he wants? Together?"

"I don't think we should do any such thing. What he wants is gross. It's clearly a turn-on for him. Do you think you should be doing anything to turn a man on?"

He chuckled. "If you think that would be going too far then it's probably going too far. Sorry, I mentioned it. If you don't want to go the prankster route, then you should just tell him that you're not going to do his date and you don't care what they do to me. I certainly don't need to work with anyone from his production company. I have other gigs, other side-jobs, and besides, if I was ever really desperate, I could teach music."

"Could you?"

"I wouldn't want to, but I could."

"Fletch," I said slowly. "I saw you at the concert, and you looked really happy when you were playing with Blades and Blasters. You did not look like that when you played for the ballet. Are you sure you're living your life the way you want to?"

He reached across the table and cupped my hand in his. "I'm sure. I've known Chase a long time and I do not want to fall deeper into that world."

"Yet, you let Rin give you that makeover?"

"Free haircut," he yawned.

I looked down and reluctantly opened the wrapping of my sandwich.

"Besides," he said, taking advantage of my moment of silence. "My mother has invited the two of us over for dinner next Sunday."

"She has?"

Fletch nodded. "I'm a little spooked about it. I'd almost rather take Carver on a date."

I shook my head. "Don't say that."

Chapter Twenty
The Mother of Wolves

Fletch

I leaned against my wreck of a car and waited for Shannon to come downstairs. When she finally appeared, I thought it was a joke. She was wearing a print dress with a ruffle around the edge. It was a wrap dress that looked perfect for a country picnic. She wore a white tank top under to shield anyone from an accidental view of her chest. Her hair was curled and was pulled out of her face in two half ponytails tied with ribbon on either side of her head. Immediately, my eyes jumped to the hem of her skirt. Was she wearing cowboy boots? She wasn't. She was wearing wedges that tied with little bows in the back.

"Just as a head's up," I said. "Simon will probably be at this dinner. Are you going to be able to face him in that getup?"

She flicked her hair off her shoulder. "Simon still doesn't know me. Perhaps this is a little more country than how I used to dress around him, but not a lot more. I have heaps of clothes that play to the same melody as the gemstones and mirrors on my walls. I only go out to meet men I really like in pleather pants and red lipstick."

She hesitated on the walkway before joining me by the side of the car.

"What?"

"You don't think I look good?" she asked shyly.

"You do, but you look a little like you're playing a part in a play. Do you really own a lot of clothes like that?"

"If I don't impress your mother…"

"Then you don't impress my mother. It's been a long time since I've lived at home." Suddenly, I stopped in my tracks. "Simon told you something about my mother, didn't he?"

Shannon looked away. "Your mother is his Aunt Beverly, isn't she?"

I nodded.

"Then, yeah, he told me a lot about her."

I did not facepalm myself. I calmly opened the car door for Shannon and closed it after her.

***

Like Shannon, I did not bring my dates home for my mother to meet. I knew that meeting my mother would only confuse the woman I wanted to date. If the woman I was seeing loved my mum, it would become a stroke in my favor and if she didn't, it would become a stroke against me. I didn't want to add my mother to the equation of whether or not a woman wanted to be with me. I wanted whatever happened between us to be between us, not between me, her, and my mother.

On the drive over, I almost took an exit to take Shannon to a drive-thru rather than take her home for dinner.

"Should we have brought rolls or something?" Shannon asked blankly.

"There's a cake I picked up from a bakery in the back."

We pulled up the long driveway and saw my brother Finn and Simon's brother Jep tossing around a football in the front yard. I got out of the car and Jep yelled, "Think fast" and threw the football at my head.

I caught it and hurled it back to him. "Don't throw that at me until I get my woman in the house."

Shannon's appeal was summed up in the effect she had on Jep and Finn. They stared at her open-mouthed as she came out of the car like she was an exotic bird flying from its cage.

Without saying hello, Jep muttered, "No wonder Simon is pissed."

"Is he here?"

They nodded in unison, as I made introductions. She got the cake I had forgotten all about, charmed them with a flip of her hair, and a minute later, I led her up the front steps.

I knew my father was impressed when he saw her. The clothes she was wearing weren't as awkward as I originally feared. She was used to wearing them and wore them with ease. Even the ribbons in her hair seemed natural.

My mother came around the corner and looked at the two of us, confused. "Where's Simon?" she questioned. "He should have told me if he was going to bring a date."

"Mum, this is Shannon. She's my girlfriend now."

"Ah, yes," my mum said as she adjusted the apron around her waist. "You're the girl Fletch was fooling around with in that picture on Facebook," she said.

Shannon's face didn't even register that she had heard my mother speak. "We brought you a cake. Is there anything I can help you with in the kitchen?"

My mother looked through the clear plastic at the cake like it was the ugliest, ickiest cake she'd ever seen. Shannon held it up and kept her face a mask of calm.

"Well, I suppose we can find a place for it, somewhere near the back. As for helping me with the dinner, everything's all taken care of, but you and Fletch can bring in some firewood if you're so bent on helping." She took the cake and disappeared back around the corner toward the kitchen.

The beautiful expression Shannon had been holding on her face abruptly fell. She stared after my mother with tight conviction marked on her face.

I took her hand and led her out the back of the house. "The firewood is back here," I said, dragging her after me.

Outside, in the cool of the backyard, I muttered, "I'm sorry. I didn't think she'd react so poorly to you. She didn't even say hello. If you'd like, we can leave right now. I don't know what Simon told her about you, but I think I'll have a word with him later about it."

She shook off my hand and sat on the woodpile. "Fletch, please relax. I have been introduced to many mothers and some of them like me and some of them don't."

"Do you know what makes the difference?"

"What I'm about to say is strange, but from my experience, it's true."

"What?"

Shannon cleared her throat. "The mothers who are glamorous and loud, they like me, and the proper ones don't."

I choked a laugh. "You must be joking."

"I wish it was a joke. Your mom looks like the poster matriarch for country living. I tried to dress like that, but it isn't enough. Not when I have Simon's scalp on my belt. Your mom probably never played with a man in her life. She probably doesn't understand the rules of those games and has always looked down on the women who play them. It's amazing how many women don't like other women because they like men, are interested in them, know how to please them, and so forth. I've had a lot of that hate. The thing is, it drives me away from other women and makes me want to be with the men who accept me, which makes the women even angrier. It's a vicious cycle."

"You have a lot of experience with this?"

"Yep. Lots of practice being disliked for my appearance and charm," she said, getting up and stretching her arms. "I can do this."

"Have you ever won over a mother who felt that way about you?"

She rubbed her temples. "No. Sometimes they convince their sons to dump me."

"I wouldn't have thought you got dumped often."

"It's happened a few times. If it's over something like this, I tend to be able to let it go. After all, if a guy who can't tell his own mother what he wants, he must not want it very much."

I watched her in the sunlight. The fabric of her dress moving over the troublesome curves of her body. The skirt fluttered in the wind and opened to show a slit up to her thigh. Why had I brought her here today? It seemed like a terrible misuse of time when there were only so many hours in a weekend. She bent to pick up a log. My hand caught her wrist before she touched one.

"Leave it. Picking up chopped logs without gloves is a good way to get a sliver. Your arms are bare. I'll get it."

Back inside, I stacked the logs next to the fireplace and heard my mother call us to the table. She sent Shannon to get Finn and Jeb from the front lawn like she was a maid who had served my family for twenty years. Shannon went and was more effective than any other person had ever been at getting the younger men into the house. They were like fishermen jumping into the ocean at the sound of a siren's call.

The table was lined up with Shannon and me on one side, Jeb, Finn, and Simon on the other side, with my mother and father at the ends. I had expected trouble from Simon, but he merely averted his eyes like he wasn't thinking about Shannon. The boys and my father were curious. They asked her where she grew up, what she did for a living, where she lived, where she had gone to school, and where she went to church.

Many of the questions were ones I'd never asked her. It wasn't that I wasn't interested in the tiniest details about her. It was that I didn't want to bore her. It was subtle, but she was showing signs of boredom and fatigue. They were exhausting her.

Or maybe it was my mother with her critical stare.

"What are your hobbies?" my mother suddenly asked.

"I like to go to the library," Shannon answered demurely.

"So, you like to read?"

"Shannon has a very interesting collection of books," Simon interjected. "My favorite one was *The Scientist's Cure for Lovesickness.*"

"Really? What was his cure?" my mother asked, raising her goblet.

"It wasn't written by a real scientist," Shannon explained.

My mother's laugh was tinny and tinkling. "Of course not."

"I mean, it's a novel. That's just the name of it. It's about a botanist who falls in love with an unknown person who designs the most beautiful tea rose. She's smitten. Through some careful investigation, she discovers who made the rose that was more perfect than any other."

"Who was it?" my father asked kindly.

"It was an old man… her father. The love she felt was not romantic. She didn't know him. She just loved his work and longed to learn more about him. She had never known her father, nor had she thought that there might be some kind of love between them. For those who long for love from unachievable heights, it's a story of hope. You might not get romantic love, but you will get unique love."

She glanced at Simon like the story meant something to the both of them.

Simon's shoulders slumped. The table had become a place of deathly stillness. Not even my mother moved or spoke. Slowly, he said, "You defeat me."

I stared at the two of them. In her own way, she had offered him a love that had nothing to do with romance and he was saying he was willing to take it. I wondered though. I wondered what he had told my mother that had made her treat Shannon

like a hostile force. I wondered where the book they were
talking about was. It was no longer on her bookshelf and she
didn't lend out her books.

Chapter Twenty One
The Mother of the Woodsman

Fletch

After dinner, I shut myself in the library with my mother while the rest of the company sat in the great room. I did want to talk to Simon as well, but I was less annoyed with him. Whatever he said about Shannon, it clearly came from a place of pain. I didn't want to be hard on him. The fact was, I could become a partaker of that particular pain with a few well-placed words from Shannon at any time.

What was happening with my mother was different. I had done the thing I didn't want to do. I had made my mother part of the equation. If Shannon got me, she also got my mother. Her unwelcome behavior had to be addressed and immediately.

"Let's talk," I said to her, drawing her away and closing the doors tight behind us. "I need you to explain to me what's going on. You don't even know Shannon and your hostility toward her has been unfathomable. You've never spoken to a guest of mine like this before. What's wrong?"

"For starters, she brought that awful cake. How am I supposed to serve that? I made a trifle. I'll serve that instead."

My expression dropped to bored. "I brought the cake, mum. She didn't pick it. I did."

"Why are you picking such terrible baked goods? Didn't I teach you better?"

"It's a chocolate cake. You like chocolate. I didn't think about it more than that. I didn't think I needed to because I've never been scolded that I brought the wrong thing to dinner before."

"I can see I need to teach you more about piping," she said stiffly.

I took her hand. "What else?"

"I hate your haircut. Doubtless, you got it because of her. You look just like those terrible hipsters on TV. Why don't you shave? Your facial hair is completely out of control. It's curling down your neck and you look like a--"

"A man?" I supplied for her. "Instead of a little boy?"

She bit back. "You look untidy."

"Let me unpick this for you. My haircut was not influenced by Shannon in the least. I was drumming last weekend and someone suggested I needed a haircut. This was what came of it. In case you were planning on blaming her, my beard has nothing to do with her either. I haven't shaved because my face has been raw lately and I was giving it a break over the weekend. I was planning to shave tomorrow."

"Oh?"

"My hair will grow out. It's just hair. That's what you say every time someone gets butchered at the salon. You laugh about it. What's really going on?"

She took a deep breath. "She's not my kind of girl."

"What does that mean?"

"She's not a girl's girl. She's a maneater. How am I supposed to have a relationship with a woman who thinks my little boy is her plaything? How is she supposed to be part of the family if the boys won't stop gawking at her and her little dress that is supposed to go down to her ankles but parts and shows her whole leg whenever she wants? She's not fooling anyone with those ribbons in her hair."

I was thinking of how to answer this sensitively when Simon burst into the room. "Sorry. I was listening at the door.

"Simon!" she squeaked. "It's really bad manners to listen at doors."

"But I have to tell you something," he said, closing the door behind him. "Shannon has three sisters and a sister-in-law. She's close with all of them. She's more of a girl's girl than you're giving her credit for. She's just scared."

"What do you mean, she's scared? I'd bet money that the girl has dragon scales on her back."

Simon lit up his phone screen and started searching for something. "Look, Auntie, you're making her into something she's not. She's just not exactly like the girls were in your day and your sons don't bring enough girls home with them for you to know the difference between a flower and a weed. You didn't get any daughters or nieces, so you don't know what Fletch brought home. This is the woman whose band he played with last weekend."

For a second, I felt like I had been hit with a sledgehammer as Simon showed my mother a picture from the Blades and Blasters' concert. It was of me and Rin. Her abdomen was showing along with her belly chain and her belly rings. There were tattoos, her wildly dyed hair, her much-too-much stage makeup, and her tongue out. Beside her was me, shirtless, while Rin wrote the words 'Wild at Heart' over my pec with her eyeliner pencil surrounded by a crowd of concertgoers.

"For frick's sake!" I exclaimed. "Someone took a picture of that?"

"It's on the Blades and Blasters' page and the Eloquent Spider's page," he explained calmly.

I looked at my mother through parted fingers.

Her teeth were clenched and she was glaring at me. "Where was Shannon during this?"

"At home, I think. She didn't come the first night. I washed all that off after I got home."

"U-huh. You know, as a parent, you sacrifice and you sacrifice. I paid for all the different rental instruments. Every time you wanted to take up the oboe or the guitar, I went to the shop and rented you the new instrument. I drove you to every band practice until you could drive yourself. I went to all your concerts, and you know how much money your father and I gave you for your university education. I would not have done any of that if I thought for one second that you would join a band!"

I stared at her. Then I started to chuckle. "You took me to band practice, thinking that I would never join a band?"

"Well, not a band like that!" she fumed.

I couldn't hold back the laughter. "Mum. That gig was a one-time thing, and whether you like it or not, I had a great time playing with them. They have a regular drummer. I was a replacement. That was not Shannon's scene and I was lucky she came to see me on the second night. You," I said, turning to Simon. "I hope that you're not harboring any further resentment toward me because your revenge is swift and brutal. I can't believe you showed my mother that picture."

Simon scoffed and put his phone away.

I turned back to my mother. "Mum, you're right. There's something off about Shannon. You're sensing it, but you're not able to label it. She's not acting like herself today. She wanted to impress you and thought that showing this side of herself was best because she wasn't confident enough to show you her true self all at once. Frankly, she's right. She's not what you're expecting or what you think you want in a daughter-in-law. Please understand that her behavior today was an act, but it was a good-natured lie."

"I want to say that I'll be happy with anything as long as you're happy, but I had such high hopes for the girl you brought home. You have always been such a good boy."

I pulled a tissue free from the box next to her.

She continued, "But I can see that you have a whole life I don't know about. Wild at heart?"

I scratched my head and didn't think of a reply.

"Wait a second," my mum said, as she gave real consideration to my words. "You said she wasn't what I was expecting in a daughter-in-law. Fletch," she clutched at my hand. "Are you going to marry her?"

"I love her. I already want to marry her. I'm here with her today to give you a head's up. I might come home tomorrow and tell you that I *have* married her."

Simon laughed. "Like you'd be able to get her to just marry you at the courthouse or something. Don't be ridiculous. She has to have a high-class wedding. It would probably take two years to plan."

I shook my head. "If she wanted to marry me, she'd marry me wearing a garbage bag. She's very determined when she wants something."

I looked to Simon for his reaction. His expression was strange. He wanted to defend Shannon, which was why he burst into the library defending her, yet he obviously did not believe she would choose me. He was still expecting me to be very disappointed.

Chapter Twenty Two
A Date with Guns and Gags

Shannon

After dinner at Fletch's parents' house, I didn't have anything left for anything or anybody. I had him drop me off at my apartment and leave me there. Normally, he and I extended our dates as long as we could. I had not slept over at his place since the first time. An idea had been forming in my head. It was a small idea, but it grew whenever we spent time together.

After I kicked my shoes off, I wished I had gone over to his place. He had a tub. I only had a shower stall and it was very cramped. If I wanted to soak my feet in something, I had a basin I kept under the sink, but that night I was too tired to pamper myself. I went over to the closet door that led to my bed and everything happened so fast.

Before I even registered that someone was in my bed, they had pulled me under them, covered my mouth, and handcuffed me to the iron-wrought headboard. Hearing the clack of metal on metal, I realized I had not been handcuffed with cookies.

"You were supposed to get back to me," Carver jeered. He pulled a gag from beside him on the bed and wrapped it around my face, pushing it hard into my mouth.

He was so heavy on top of me, with one of my arms pinned to my side and the other in the handcuff, I couldn't even move.

His hand moved across my body. He was looking for my phone. After a thorough pet, he realized I was still holding it in the hand that was under his knee. It was useless to scream through the gag.

He tossed my phone out the closet door and leaned his face so close to mine, I could see the pores in his nose. "Since you won't come to me, I've come to you."

Getting off me, he positioned my armchair outside the closet to stare at me. He held a gun in his hand. Convinced he had given me an adequate reason not to scream, he offered gloatingly, "You can take your gag off and we'll have a conversation."

I rolled my eyes and removed the gag with my free hand. "Dude, what do you want out of all this? If you think that it's my normal routine to cart a man away at gunpoint and that's the kind of woman you want in your life, you have to understand, that isn't me. The gun I had that night was not a real gun. The handcuffs I used were toys. Fletch was in no real danger ever. I would never put a human being in danger. This handcuff you've got around my wrist looks f-ing authentic, as does your gun. Could you stop pointing that thing at me? I'm handcuffed, so I can't run and I'm willing to talk to you without screaming. Put the gun away!"

He dropped it with a deadpan expression on his face. It fell on the floor with a thud. It was not plastic.

"Is that thing loaded?" I demanded.

"I guess that's all part of the surprise," he said, looking bored. "Why didn't you do the date like I asked you to?"

I sighed noisily from my position on my back. "I hadn't come up with a plan on how to do it," I lied because I had planned to ignore him completely. "I needed time to prepare. It took me a week to plan a dinner I made for Fletch. You didn't give me anywhere near enough time."

"Yet, I saw Fletch drop you off tonight. By your outfit, you were on a date with him. Why were you on a date with him when you were supposed to be planning a date with me? I told you what I would do to him if you didn't do what I wanted. Didn't you take me seriously?"

"You didn't tell me I had to stop seeing Fletch. I didn't say I would stop seeing him. Frankly, I'm a little more concerned about what you're going to do to me in this situation than I am over Fletch's career."

"I'm not going to do anything to you other than talk to you. I haven't got you where I want you yet."

"Yeah, what do you want?"

"I want you to beg me to do this sort of thing with you."

His voice was terrible and I felt my insides shudder in fear and disgust. "I am not a BDSM kind of girl."

"I didn't think I was into it either until I heard you say my name and haul away a different man. I felt like I had never been to a carnival, a movie theater, or woken up on Christmas morning." He leaned forward. "I felt like all the experiences in life that are supposed to be highs are actually lows. Work has always been more fun than play until I heard you give my invitation to him."

"I can't change that he was the one I picked up. I can't change that now, Carver."

"I love how you say my name."

"Mr. Criche?" I tried, hoping that would be less interesting to him.

"I may like that more," he smirked.

I threw my one hand up in exasperation. "Look, this kind of stunt is not going to get me. This kind of stunt is going to make me report you to the police and get an emergency protection order placed on you. Is that what you want?"

"I've never had a mugshot. See if you can give me a fat lip and cut my eyebrow before they haul me away, will you? I've always thought that would make a good album cover."

He was completely insane. I couldn't do anything. I couldn't reach my phone. If I started screaming, he'd just gag me again or point the gun at me until I stopped. After he'd had his fun, would he just leave? How was I going to keep living here if he could get in?

"How did you get in here?" I asked.

"That will have to be another surprise."

I groaned. "Where do you live?"

"Why? Are you gonna try to break in? A little payback?"

Instantly, I knew I could never do that. It was exactly what he wanted.

"What else are we going to do for our 'date'?" I air quoted with one hand.

"What would Fletch do?" he suddenly asked.

"He'd play music for me."

Carver grabbed his phone. "Right. I should have been playing music this whole time. Want to hear the demo for the latest band I signed?"

I wanted to say, 'Not really,' but bit my tongue on it.

He started playing a track on his phone, but to me, it didn't sound like anything. It was music that was so much like everything else I'd ever heard that it didn't make any impact. At the least, it was okay background music.

"Then what would he do?"

Examining Carver's face, I realized he did not know anything about the world he was trying to enter. He would probably do anything I asked him to. I did a little prioritizing in my head. My long-term goal was to get him out of my life. My short-term goal was to get him out of my apartment. While I was so powerless, I was going to need to satisfy him.

"He would give me a pedicure," I lied, thinking of how sore my feet still were. "He hasn't given me one in two weeks."

Carver looked stunned. "I've never done that for anyone. I don't know if I know how."

"Stop being a loser, look up instructions on your phone and I'll tell you where I keep my supplies."

All in all, it took him an hour and a half to give me a pedicure according to the directions he'd found. I sent him to find my basin, my exfoliator, my bubble bath, my manicure set, and my lotion. He sat on the floor timing how long my feet had been soaking with his white shirt sleeves rolled up and his legs crossed. It would have been cute if my wrist was not still in the handcuff.

I hoped he would be disgusted by the amount of skin that came off, but he didn't seem to notice the way I did when I did it myself. I also hoped he would be annoyed at how often I 'accidentally' splashed him. But by the time he was doing my nails I had pretty much lost hope that he wouldn't enjoy every step of the process.

Carver had a great time, even though I thought the idea of giving another human being a pedicure was mildly repulsive. If Fletch had told me he wanted me to give him one for one of our dates, I would have suggested that instead of a pedicure he let me write something on the bottom of his foot with a ballpoint pen to see how much he squirmed and if he could figure out what I was writing. That would have been much more interesting to me.

When Carver put the last coat of polish on my toenails, he happened to glance at his phone and see the time. "I have to go," he said as he screwed the lid of the topcoat back on. He picked up his gun, his coat and prepared to leave.

"Aren't you going to undo my handcuffs?"

He blew me a kiss from the open apartment door. "No. I think you can get out of them if you try."

I screamed that he shouldn't leave me like that, but he locked the doorknob and closed the door.

Fuming, I sat there stupidly for a few minutes, waiting for the toenail polish to dry. When it was, I pulled out the toe separator and checked out the handcuffs more carefully. They weren't toys bought from a toyshop, but they weren't on the same level as the ones Officer Todd wore at his belt. I bet he'd bought them at a love shop and he'd cut the fur muffs off them.

First I tried to squirm out of the cuff. Then I tried to twist the mechanism inside so it would hopefully give way. Neither worked. Annoyed, I tried to reach under my bed. That was where I kept my vandalism supplies and I had a pair of bolt cutters down there. Bending over as far as I could, I still couldn't reach them.

Angier than I had ever been, I lifted up my whole mattress and kicked it out of my closet. I didn't have a box spring, so I reached between the slats and pulled out my bolt cutters. I had to work them one side of a link at a time, one-handed, with my feet stuck through the slats and resting on the carpet beneath. If they had been higher quality handcuffs, I wouldn't have been able to do it.

I was free.

Ripping my apartment apart, I retrieved my phone from under the mattress and called my landlord.

He picked up the phone and I shouted, "I'm having a big problem, Eric!"

He grumbled and then got off his butt.

Chapter Twenty Three
What I See Versus what I Hear

Fletch

I had just come from an audition at the theater. There was a new play coming out and they needed a talented percussionist to play tinkling sounds for dramatic emphasis to let the audience know that the ghost of the main character's dead wife was nearby. They were choosing between me and two other percussionists I knew. One of them I even played with in the orchestra. In the past, when he and I auditioned for the same part, it was a close call between which one of us would get it. This time, I knew I'd gotten the part before I left. If I wanted it.

The director of the play had been at the Blades and Blasters concert and seen me perform. She had stars in her eyes and the way she looked me up and down felt like sexual harassment. Now I wasn't sure if I wanted the part.

I had to make it back to the music shop. I'd taken time off to go to the audition, which was one of the perks of working at the music shop. They were cool about letting me go when I had an audition. That was the life of a musician.

I was just passing the Greek restaurant I had taken Shannon to on our first date. I looked across the street to reminisce about the sweet sound and sight of the bracelets at her wrist.

That was when I saw her. She was standing in front of the restaurant talking to Officer Todd. She was leaning against the brick wall and Todd was very close to her. Whatever she was talking to him about, his jaw was set, and her face was the perfect picture of anguish. If I were a passer-by who didn't know Shannon and Todd, I would think that she was breaking up with him, or he was breaking up with her.

Still, I stopped in my tracks and watched them.

What was going on?

It didn't look like Officer Todd was reprimanding her. It looked like he was a heartbeat away from putting his arm around her shoulders and drawing her close to him. He was listening to her talk intently and then he licked his lower lip.

I put out my foot to cross the street when my phone rang noisily in my pocket. I took the call. "Hey," I said.

"Hey," Rin said in her languid I-don't-care voice. "How are things? I hope they're cool. I want to talk to you about a gig."

"I thought Blades and Blasters had moved on to Calgary," I said, keeping my eyes on Shannon and Officer Todd.

"We did, except my little sister's band is playing at the Eloquent Spider this Wednesday night and she needs someone to cover drums. I told her you were there and you were amazing and she should get you to come in. I'm coming too. She needs a backup singer and a guitarist. I said I'd throw on a wig and help."

"I don't get it. Aren't you on tour? Are you free to run back and forth doing little favors for people? Aren't you supposed to be concentrating on making your show in Vancouver next week a success?"

"Yeah, I should be… but the thing is… I'm not really coming back for her show. I'm using her show as an excuse. I'm coming to get you."

"Really?" I asked with an unconscious smack of my lips.
"Why?"

"My drummer is a shit. He keeps drinking too much and getting into accidents. He hit his head last night. I don't know how long I can have you on tour, but if you're willing to cover for him, I can offer you work for the rest of the tour."

"I'll bet if you used a drum machine, no one in the audience would notice or care, Rin. I can't go on tour with you. I have stuff here I am dealing with."

Across the street, Shannon had begun screaming and swearing and Officer Todd had put his arms around her in an obvious attempt to calm her down. They were about one pose off looking exactly like the picture Shannon and I had taken against the brick wall.

But Rin snapped my attention back to her. "If you're worried about money, I promise I can pay you as much as your job and more. You and your six-pack will bring out more in an audience than a drum machine."

"I thought Carver didn't want you or anyone else he was producing to hire me anymore," I retorted.

Her voice was slow. "Yeah, he said he didn't want me to hire you, but he won't be at any of our shows, and last week you turned our audience into a pack of raving beasts. I've always dreamed of singing for a crowd that was that psyched. Come on, Fletcher Litman. Don't let me down."

I groaned. "It doesn't sound like I have any time to think about this."

"No. You do. It's only Monday. I'll see you when I get there tomorrow. I'll convince you then."

We said good-bye and hung up, but when I looked across the street to see what had become of Shannon and Officer Todd, they were gone.

Chapter Twenty Four
The Dress Test

Shannon

Notices had been coming up on my social media. Fletch was going to play at the Eloquent Spider with a band called Windstorm and I had been battered with information about it.

In response, I wrote Fletch a saucy text asking him if he would be performing shirtless again, to which he sent me a picture of the clothes he would be wearing. To be clear, he only sent a picture of the clothes hung on a hanger. It was a black wife-beater and black cargo pants.

I guessed that if I wanted to see him in them, I had to go to the show.

The show was that night, so that morning I asked Levi about the thing that was really bothering me. "Do you know if Carver Criche has a particular connection to the Eloquent Spider?"

Levi scratched the stubble on his chin. "Well, he books the place for his bands to play at. If he thinks he can get more people coming, he books a bigger hall, like the Sunspear center, but the Eloquent Spider is a good place for the little bands to start."

"Ever heard of a band called Windstorm?"

"Nope. I only hear about the ones that have recording contracts."

I nodded. That was just like Levi. He didn't worry about anything except what work paid well. Along those lines, I had seen that Natalie had paid all her outstanding fees with him, so he was in a particularly good mood. I hadn't realized it before, but he had thought that Natalie was going nowhere with her talent. He had never expected her to pay him. If that was how he felt, why had he let her accrue all those hours?

I was about to ask when the front door opened and a delivery man came in. He had a package. I signed for it before I saw it was for me.

"I didn't think you got things delivered to the office," Levi said, trying to sneak a peek at what it could be before I tore open the flap.

"I don't get anything delivered," I replied. "I don't have room in my place for anything."

The enormous envelope was very plain and I pulled a piece of black fabric out of it.

"What is it?"

I pulled it between my fingers. "It's a dress."

"There's a note attached," Levi said, grabbing the hem of the garment as it flapped around. "See you at the show," he read.

"Oh. It's from Fletch," I said as I looked at the return address. "I guess he wants me to wear it tonight."

Levi made a clicking noise with his tongue and excused himself.

***

I tried the dress on after work.

It had a turtleneck, extended shoulder sleeves, and hugged my body tightly until just above my knee. Actually, it was too tight. It scratched at my neck. I tried to wear a slip under it to protect me from the uncomfortable seams, but it didn't look right. The dress was too tight and showed every seam and line in my slip. I hadn't realized there was so much lace around the hem of my slip before because it had never been an issue when I wore it under any of my other dresses.

I took off the dress, removed my slip, shook my head sadly, and put the dress back on. If I liked Fletch less, I wouldn't have worn it.

All the same, I put on some knee-high boots and hoped that it wouldn't be too cold out that night.

***

At the club, I texted Fletch when I was outside. It was about ten minutes before his show. I had meant to be there sooner, but I refused to walk to the Eloquent Spider in the dress that felt like paper, and it took forever for a cab to come.

When I got there, there wasn't an oppressive line of people waiting outside since Windstorm was a lesser band than Blades and Blasters. I started to feel guilty about Fletch coming to let me skip the door fee, and sauntered up to the entrance. Besides, it was too cold to wait outside.

Once inside, I was surprised at how full the dance floor was. I hadn't expected anyone to be inside after the sparse splattering of people outside. I guessed they'd come early.

Fletch met me on the edge of the dance floor.

"Baby," he said, pulling me into an embrace. "You look beautiful."

I was about to say something about how I'd better look good and thank him for the dress when Ringlet came up behind Fletch and grabbed him by the Y strap on his back.

"No chatting," she barked without looking at me. "Sissy's friend has no idea how to set up a drum kit and if you don't get the cymbals on right, they'll probably come off."

He moved to kiss me, but the force of Ringlet's hoist moved him out of the space of even my fingers.

If he'd had a pair of earplugs with him, he hadn't had a chance to give them to me. I shrugged and pulled a fresh pair out of my bag. As I finished twisting them into my ears, I noticed a few kids watching me from the bench of a booth. Not only was I alone, but I was also putting in earplugs like a snob.

I needed a seat.

I watched Windstorm play for two minutes before I got bored. Why were there so many people at the club to see them? Levi didn't always get contracts from the best artists, but the only proper thing that was happening on that stage was Fletch's drumming. Even Ringlet's guitar skills and backup singing left much to be desired.

I wondered if they were planning to play more than one set as I approached the bar, which was empty with most people back on the dancefloor.

I sat on a stool.

"Got anything hot?" I asked as I sat down.

"I can make you something hot," the bartender offered with that look on his face that I was more than familiar with. There was no one else at the bar and he thought it was his lucky day. He'd serve me drinks and we were far enough away from the sound of the band playing that he could have a little banter with me.

The look of pleasure on his face deflated me. In the past, I would have taken full advantage of a man's willingness to go out of his way for me, but tonight, it just made me feel out of place in my own skin.

"Do you like chocolate or peaches? I know a really good recipe for mulled peach wine."

That sounded like it would take forever. "Actually, I haven't had anything to eat and if I drink that, I'll feel worse. I'd like orange juice and soda. "

"What's making you feel bad?" he asked, taking my money and pulling on his soda handle.

"This dress. This music."

The bartender laughed.

Suddenly, two guys took the seats on either side of me. They were enormous and practically crushing me between them even though the stools were screwed to the floor.

Sitting between them was horribly uncomfortable, and I moved to leave once the bartender was finished making my drink.

"Oh, don't go darling," one of the hulking men said. "We don't mean to chase you off. We're just here to talk for a minute."

I paused, wondering how badly I would offend them if I strode away with my nose in the air and what the consequences of that might be.

"These guys are the bouncers," the bartender informed me. "They'll just be a minute."

I put my weight back on my stool. Besides, as I looked behind me, the bar was starting to fill up.

I pulled at my collar.

I was uncomfortable. It wasn't just the dress. What was I doing? This was exactly the sort of thing I had rejected Simon over. I even told Fletch on that first night when we were handcuffed together that I wouldn't be the girl who was hauled to sleazy clubs, and now I had been hauled to this sleazy club twice. What was I doing?

I knew damn well what I was doing. I was waiting for Fletch to finish his drumming so he would take me to a quiet Greek restaurant and then I would make him feed me pita bread with hummus. Sometimes sets were only twenty minutes. They were probably halfway finished already, but I was going out of my mind.

The reason I didn't jump up from my chair was that it had gone from six degrees celsius to forty-two degrees in a matter of minutes. I was boiling, and the bouncers weren't leaving. The juice was sour, and my dress was chafing my neck.

Okay, I liked Fletch.

I was in love with Fletch.

That was the only reason I was putting up with this crap.

And I wouldn't put up with it anymore. He wanted to know the real me? Well, he was going to get the real me that night. I was going to tell him what I thought of the Eloquent Spider and the people who worked there and the people who worked with the people who worked there. I was going to tell him not to send me pretty dresses because I had so many sensory issues that he was forbidden to shop for me.

I stood up.

I was leaving and when he bothered to contact me, he'd find out why.

I stormed out to the lobby with my fingers in my collar, angry and uncomfortable when I noticed something. When I pulled my fingers out of my collar, there were black smudges on them. It was exactly like I had had my fingerprints taken at the police station, except the ink was on the front and back of all my fingers except my pinkie.

Stunned, I pushed my way into the women's bathroom.

Looking at myself in the mirror, I pulled my collar down. Black was smudged in a thick ring around my throat. That was not the handiwork of the cheapest fabric and the cheapest dye in the world. Something was going on.

I checked the bathroom stalls, and when I saw that I was alone, I ripped the dress over my head. There was ink all over my body. Like an enormous inky typewriter had used me as its paper, I had the words, "I want Carver" written all over where the dress had touched me, except where my underwear had protected me. I put my hand under the soap pump and smeared some soup on my chest where the words were the clearest. I yanked at the paper towel roll and wetted it.

The only thing that happened was that I got my bra wet.

The words were not coming off.

Fletch hadn't sent me the dress. Carver had. He had somehow used permanent ink and I didn't know when it would ever come off.

I called Todd.

"What's up, Shannon?" he asked pleasantly.

"Where are you? I'm at the Eloquent Spider and I really need you to come get me," I was not going to cry, but my voice quivered over the phone.

"Why? Is someone chasing you?"

"No. I have a huge problem. I need help, and you are the only one who can help me right now."

"I'm just down the block," he said. "I'll be there in a minute."

"Okay. I'm in the girl's room."

He was faster than I imagined and I was still wiping at the ink hopelessly when he came in.

He looked at me, up and down. Then up and down again. I could tell he was struggling desperately to stay professional. If I had been a random person he didn't know, he wouldn't have struggled at all. Instead, his blue eyes flashed like he was seeing something he should never see on duty. Then he chuckled. "What happened? Did someone do this to you when you were drunk?"

"When have I ever been drunk, Todd? Someone pulled a prank on me."

"Who?"

I tugged at my bra straps to emphasize Carver's name across my cleavage.

"Was it the same guy who made you submit to a pedicure at gunpoint?"

I shook my head wearily, before shouting at him, "If you laugh again, I swear I'll kill you. That wasn't funny, and neither is this!"

"Okay, I'll go get a camera, so we can take some pictures of this, and an evidence bag, so I can take that dress. Maybe some clothes for you," he said, before ducking out of the ladies' room.

I didn't like the way he said *maybe*.

Chapter Twenty Five
A Woman with Words in All the Right Places

Fletch

I walked around the front of the Eloquent Spider, but I couldn't see Shannon anywhere. There were a few minutes between sets that I could spend with her, but she was nowhere to be seen. I approached the bar, confused. I had texted her as soon as I finished, but she hadn't answered. I checked my phone again.

"What's up, Fletch?" Bradford said as I approached the bar. "I hear Rin is picking up your drinks for the night, so what are you having?"

"Just give me a bottle of water. I'm too hot for anything."

"Drumming shirtless is better, huh?" the bartender quipped, as he fetched my water from a glass cooler behind him. "You look confused. What's wrong?"

"I'm looking for a woman. Maybe you've seen her. She was wearing a black dress that came up to her chin."

Bradford nodded, licking his lips playfully and enjoying what he was about to say. "Yeah. I've seen her. She went into the ladies' room and a man went in after her. They haven't come out yet."

I squinted at him disbelievingly. "Am I supposed to bust in the girl's bathroom now?"

He smiled broadly. "I'll come with you if you want backup."

"Aren't you supposed to be minding the bar?"

"It'll only take a second. It would take me longer to go to the back for a new bag of wine. Let's go."

I was about to tell him to go soak his head when I remembered the true nature behind Shannon's pretenses. I didn't know where her limits were or what she would or wouldn't do. I didn't think she was fooling around behind my back at the bathroom during my show. That made no sense, but the idea that she could be up to no good made perfect sense. Had she found some trouble?

"Wait," I said, putting my hand up to stop Bradford, who had just come around the bar. "I'll go check it out myself. It's okay. I've been thrown into girl's bathrooms before."

"Suit yourself," Bradford called after me as I strode toward the bathroom.

I opened the door a crack and I heard a male voice say, "You look like a model, Shannon. If you look too hot, these pictures are going to turn out all wrong." He paused and I opened the door enough to see inside. Officer Todd had a huge digital camera in his hands and he was looking at the pictures he'd taken. "These are all terrible. You have to look sad. Nevermind. I'll start by getting close-ups."

I pushed the door open the rest of the way and saw Shannon. She was wearing only her black bra, panties, and knee-high boots. There was writing all over her chest, back, and thighs. Her neck was entirely stained black, and Todd was completely right about how she looked… upsettingly sexy.

"What's going on?" I asked, not feeling like I was walking in on anything I shouldn't.

"Fletch?" Shannon squeaked, her face turning bright red and horrified.

"That's the look we're going for," Todd exclaimed before shooting off twenty shots of her red face as she wrung her hands and stared at me appealingly.

"I want Carver," I read off of her thigh.

Todd's calm, authoritative voice chimed in. "He put ink inside this dress. From what I can tell, he sent it to her intending to deceive her so she thought the dress came from you. Shannon says she thought your apartment was the return address on the package, but anyone could have put that on. It seems that her sweat activated the ink. It doesn't come off with water. Hell of a prank, eh?"

"He did this?" I asked, looking at her alarmed face. She had black smudges on her fingers and when she put a hand to her mouth, it came off on her cheeks. I had never seen her so alarmed. I read it again, "I want Carver. Yeah, I want Carver all right." I turned around and the only thought in my head was booting it upstairs to see if he was in the VIP room with Chase.

Shannon put her hand on my shoulder to stop me from going and then withdrew it lightning-fast because she'd smeared my shoulder with ink. "Sorry! But please stay," she cried. "Or, maybe don't go get in a fistfight. Todd went to get me some clothes when he went to get the camera, but he didn't have any. Do you have anything with you that I can wear so that I can leave?"

"Shannon, you know I'd give you the shirt off my back," I said, pulling the wife-beater off and handing it to her.

She took it gratefully and slid it over her head. Wearing it, she looked like an album cover. I kicked off my shoes and undid the button on the cargo pants.

"You don't have to take those off too," she said, seeing the top of my blue and white striped boxer shorts.

"Because I'll look silly walking through the club? I'm debating whether or not I should still drum the second set in my underwear." I pretended to contemplate this. "Nah. It would never work."

"You can play, or not, but keep your pants on!" she almost shrieked. Then she calmed down and said, "Look, this shirt hits me mid-thigh. Todd can give me a ride home and I'll be okay. I just need this shirt."

Todd had finished taking pictures. "Shannon, do you want to come to the station to make your statement tonight or do you want to come in tomorrow?"

"Tonight!"

"Great. Let's go. I'll turn on the heat in the cruiser."

Feeling helpless as Todd handed Shannon his jacket, I put my hands in my pockets. I felt my keys jingle. "Wait," I called. "Shannon, don't go home after you go to the police station. Go to my apartment."

"Why?"

"Because I have a tub and you don't. I'll pick up some things to help you get the ink off and meet you there."

Tearfully, she took the keys, tucked them into her purse, and left with Officer Todd. He gave me an approving nod and they stepped into the entrance of the club.

Rin met me in the lobby as I watched Shannon and Todd drive away.

"Just can't keep a shirt on you, huh?" she said with a flirtatious smack of her lips.

I turned to her. "What do you know about that?"

"About Shannon Bilx getting hauled off in a police car? Nothing. I didn't know they let criminals ride in the front."

I didn't think that anyone in the world knew that Shannon was a criminal. I didn't let Rin's brazen accusation fluster me. "So, Carver didn't want me to perform with you tonight?"

"Yup. Good thing he's not here."

"I bet he is here," I said slowly. "I bet he's the one who suggested that you hire me for your tour and that he told you to hire me tonight too. Your sister's band is crap and yet this place is packed, and it's not packed with nobodies. I spotted a few local big wigs in the audience. You and your sister had better hope that there's no such thing as bad publicity, otherwise, this show might haunt your careers."

"They came as a special favor to Carver," she said, before flinching.

"Wish you could bite your tongue off?" I questioned as I regarded the people loitering on the edges of the dancefloor.

"I didn't mean to say that. I meant to say that they're here as a special favor to me. You know, because I'm so famous."

"Do you know what Carver did to Shannon tonight? Why she's getting taken away in a police car?"

Rin paled and her eyes widened.

"Look," I continued. "I don't know if your offer for me to join your band was authentic or not--"

"It is," she interrupted.

I put up my hand to stop her from saying more. "I don't know if it was a real offer, but I have to refuse. Don't bother ever looking me up again. Playing with your band those two nights was fun, but it wasn't fun enough to have to deal with Carver or anyone connected to him. For the second set, either ask Chase to cover for me or get him to get one of his goons to hook up a drum machine."

"Wait! You'll never play with me again? Isn't that being a little too rash? I mean, we're all in this music industry together. We're not competing. We can work together and… I don't want to see you go."

I rubbed the spot between my eyebrows. "What do you care? You're willing to play their little games, so go play."

I strolled out the Eloquent Spider without my shirt on into the cold night air. I walked two steps toward my car before I realized that I couldn't even drive it home. I had given my keys to Shannon.

Chapter Twenty Six
Bathtub of Dreams

Shannon

I had bubbles up to my eyebrows when Fletch returned to his apartment. I didn't see him at first because of all the bubbles. He was racing around frantically.

"Fletch!" I called to him over the mountain of bubbles. "Is everything okay?"

"Everything is fine. I just need to get my keys and run down to the drug store. I'll be back before your bath cools." The door slammed.

By the time he returned, I had almost dropped his copy of *Creating a Xylophone Soundscape* into the bathwater three times, and the bubbles had considerably come down.

"I'm back," he shouted, "and I've brought three types of cures for ink on skin."

"I had a lot of success getting it off my legs, chest, and stomach, but there's nothing I can do about my back," I replied.

He got a clean towel and draped it over the edge of the tub. "Lean on that and I'll scrub your back," he offered.

I unhooked my bra and leaned my chest against the towel while he rubbed baby oil into my back.

"Are you really upset?" he asked.

"Yup," I replied through gritted teeth. It wasn't really that I felt as savage as that sounded. I just felt like I was on the verge of crying again and I didn't want to cry. Carver had pulled a practical joke on me. This wasn't even the first time I'd had an ink-style practical joke played on me. I should have been tougher. What was making me into such a baby that night?

"Is it coming off?" I questioned stiffly.

"Yeah. All your soaking in the tub is taking your skin off with it. Nothing to worry about. Just a bit of healthy exfoliation."

"You sound so cheerful," I moaned as I glanced over my shoulder. Unless I was mistaken, he had that expression on his face the night I kidnapped him. For the first time, I wondered if that look didn't mean he was pleased. "Is this awkward for you?"

He shrugged. "I was just thinking that if Carver Criche had any idea that his prank would lead to me scrubbing your naked back in my bathtub, he would not have done it. This almost feels like revenge."

"Pleasant revenge?"

"Very pleasant." He grinned.

I winked back at him before turning my head forward and giving it a break from the strain of looking over my shoulder. "What happened after I left?"

"I quit, told Ringlet to get a drum machine, told her I would not work with her in the future and left the club with no shirt. Then I realized I'd given you my car keys, so I had to walk home."

"You mean that you were out walking with no shirt on while I was at the police station giving my statement?"

"Yes. I managed to snag a bus on the way to pick up my car and the baby oil. I also bought you some chocolates. They're only from the drugstore, but I thought you'd rather have cherry cordials and coconut white chocolate than nothing."

"Yes! Yes, I would rather have those things instead of nothing. Can I have one now?"

"Sure," he said, tossing the sponge at me before drying his oily hands on a paper towel and retrieving the chocolate from the plastic bag. He set them out in front of me on the bathmat while I added more hot water to the tub. He clicked on some soft xylophone instrumentals and took up his sponge again.

After about two minutes of eating cherry cordials, listening to chill music that barely had a melody, having my back scrubbed and massaged, I realized that this was the best date I had ever been on. I was about to tell Fletch how I felt when the door buzzer rang.

"You can't be expecting anyone!" I yelped.

"I'm not, but I am going to see who it is," he said, getting up and drying his hands a second time while the door buzzer made impatient, unpleasant noises. He clicked the button. "Who is it?"

"Chase."

"You sack of crap," Fletch replied. "What are you doing here?"

"I want to talk about Natalie," his disembodied voice answered.

Fletch looked at me as if to ask me what I wanted.

"Are we finished?" I asked, pointing at my back.

"No, but I would have stretched that out for hours," Fletch admitted with a shrug and an especially pleased grin.

"Do you have a robe I can ruin?"

"I guess that means you want me to let him up," Fletch said, pressing the button. Then he went over to his closet area and dug up a robe. "I don't think you'll ruin it. It's already black." He brought it over with a fresh towel, set them on the toilet seat where I could grab them, and turned his back.

"Are you sure you can't see a reflection of me somewhere?" I asked suspiciously from the bubbles of the tub.

"I am trying to be a gentleman, but I'm going to reach my limit soon, so get out of the water quickly. I wouldn't mind having ink spread all over my body in the least."

I had been thinking something similar. Usually, I didn't want to have sex with the men I knew. I didn't want to give them any knowledge of who I was or what I was like, in or out of my clothes. Those were things I kept to myself for good reasons.

Following his advice, I hopped out of the tub quickly, wrapped the towel around myself, and then his bathrobe over that.

"I'm finished," I said, just as the tap came at the door.

Fletch walked over to it and peered through the peephole. "Are you alone?" he asked.

"Of course, I'm alone. It's one in the morning on a weeknight. The club closes at eleven. I had to wait this long to get rid of Carver and come see you. I would have called you sooner, but the man was watching me like a hawk."

"Okay," Fletch said as he opened the door.

Chase burst in, sweaty and red-cheeked. He stopped in his tracks when he saw me. "Oh," he said, stopping to straighten his shirt. "You have company."

Fletch closed and locked the door behind Chase and offered him a seat at the kitchen table since the only other seats were the toilet or the bed. I took the bed and wrapped Fletch's blankets around me, letting the wet towel fall on the floor. Fletch scooped it up and hung it on a wall hook. Then he brought me the remaining chocolates.

"Why does she get chocolate?" Chase teased, obviously trying to lighten the mood.

"Because she's prettier than you are."

Chase was about to say something, but stopped and ran a finger sideways along his neck. He had been about to say something about how I wasn't so pretty with that ring of ink around my neck. I had tried to scrub at it, but without a mirror, I had had very little success.

He cleared his throat and said, "I feel responsible for this."

"You do?" Fletch asked quietly. "Why?"

"Because I'm the one who told Natalie that if she really wanted to get Carver's attention, she should pull a prank on him involving guns."

"How do you know Natalie?"

He balked. "I've known her for ages. She has sung at the Spider every Tuesday night for years. I don't pay her, because hardly anyone comes in on Tuesdays, but she gets the practice of playing for an audience every week, and if she was really talented, she could get a following that way."

"But she's not really talented, is she?"

"No and yes. Her voice is great. The songs she writes aren't catchy, but everything works out if she sings covers. Then, at least, people don't throw things at her. They tap their toes and wonder why she isn't famous. If singing every Tuesday could make her happy, I would f-ing marry her--"

I gasped. "You're the guy!"

"What?"

"You're the guy. When Natalie left me and Fletch in the camp kitchen, she left and went to a few places, but the place she ended up was at a man's house and she went in to stay the night. That was you!"

Chase sighed. "Yes. That was me."

"And Carver saw you, recognized you, but didn't tell me who you were when he recounted it to me."

"Yeah, and I knew that if she could get his attention with a prank, he might decide to help her. If he helped her, something might click for her. Maybe he'd set her up with a decent songwriter or something."

"Weren't you afraid he'd be so taken with her little prank that he'd fall in love with her?" I asked.

"No." Chase seemed to think the idea remarkably funny. "Even if he was very impressed, it would only last a minute. Natalie is not the type of woman who thinks on her toes. It was a stunt I designed to get his attention, so he would listen to her sing. It didn't work, but the flyers I wrote worked better, and your little lecture to him where you talked down on him and made him feel like an insecure little boy who couldn't play with the big kids. That was more than I could have hoped for. He became hyper curious, found Natalie, and became obsessed with the idea of showing you how powerful he is. Are you having fun yet?"

"So the job offer with Ringlet was all part of his scheme?" Fletch asked.

"Oh yes, but that doesn't mean that Ringlet doesn't want you. She wasn't even having problems with her drummer. They asked you to come in just so Carver could shove a wedge between the two of you. He's very jealous of you, Fletch. I've never seen anyone that jealous in my life and I work in the music industry." He pulled out a pack of cigarettes. "Can I smoke in here?"

"No," Fletch replied stonily.

"Whatever. I'm not staying long. I came to tell you that I masterminded this, but I didn't take Shannon into account. Natalie bringing Shannon along with her that night was something she thought of herself because she's not gutsy, but Shannon is. Shannon did all the hard parts. From what Natalie told me, she handled the gun, your conversation, and everything… Natalie never could have done it alone."

I thought as much.

"What's more," Chase continued, looking at me. "You're stuck with him."

"I've been reporting him to the police," I replied.

"Good. Great. You do that," Chase said, stroking the tattoo on the side of his neck. "He's going to discredit you. He's going to make it sound like everything you've said is nonsense. Remember, he's determined to show you he's the biggest man in the city."

I mulled that over.

"Is that all you have to give her after the trouble you've caused?" Fletch asked.

"I didn't tell your girlfriend to be so damn sexy that Carver Criche, who practically stamps panties for a living, can't control himself. If it had been up to me, she wouldn't have become involved."

"You think about him this way and you sent Natalie to prank him?" Fletch asked.

"But Natalie is not interesting."

"Yet you'd marry her?"

"I'd always know she wasn't cheating," Chase said, pointing an unlit cigarette at Fletch.

I put my hand up. "Stop it. I think you've given me more than enough advice. Thank you."

"See? She thinks I'm cool," Chase said, sticking a thumb out at me.

Fletch rolled his eyes.

Chase stood up to leave. "One more thing. Ringlet is heartbroken you gave her the boot. She was in the VIP lounge crying until Carver sent her back to her hotel. She'll be back begging for sure."

"Please discourage her," Fletch said with disgust on the edge of his words.

"No problem. I know lots of drummers," he said, sticking his cigarette in his mouth. "Shannon," he said, turning to me. "I'm not certain you heard the important part of what I said. Did you get what I came here to give you?"

I nodded. "More or less. He's not really after me. He wants to be the biggest man in the city?"

"Or the country."

"Or the world?" I said, giving Chase a kissy face.

Chase hooted another laugh. "Then I'll leave you two love birds to it. The man wants to be big."

Chapter Twenty Seven
The Talk

Shannon

Fletch gave me a stack of warm clothes, complete with underwear and socks. I put them on and got back into his bed. Then I told him about what happened with Carver on Sunday night after he dropped me off.

"I got the landlord to change the locks that night, otherwise, I would not have felt comfortable staying there," I explained as I shook my head. "But truthfully, the place feels gross… tainted. I started looking for a new apartment."

"Did you have any success?" Fletch asked sympathetically.

"We already live in one of the sketchiest parts of the city. I like how much I pay in rent and I think my building is one of the best ones in the area. Except that guy broke in twice. The first time, he didn't get inside my apartment. He only got into the hallway, but the second time he did. I still don't know how he got in."

"Have you thought about moving somewhere bigger and getting a roommate?"

"I'm not sure that that wouldn't ruin my life more than Carver. If I had a roommate, she'd eventually find out about my little hobbies and then I wouldn't know if I could trust her. She'd have blackmail on me whenever she wanted. Unless she was up to something pretty shady herself, I'd always be at a disadvantage. I don't know. I feel really weird about my women friends since Natalie hit me with a brick. I've known her for years and I didn't even know she was seeing Chase."

Fletch suppressed a smile. "What about living with a man?"

"He'd be trying to get down my pants constantly."

Fletch nodded. "That sounds legit, but you're not getting what I'm suggesting. Why don't you move in with me?"

"Huh?" I gasped, awestruck.

"I already know about your little hobbies and I don't condemn you for them. I would never blackmail you, although, you're very right about the pants thing." He grinned. "I would want down your pants constantly."

I bit my lip. I had never had the conversation I was about to have with Fletch with anyone, and I hadn't prepared myself. For some reason, I thought I had more time with Fletch before we had to talk. I swallowed hard. "I have a problem."

"What's that?"

"I'm not… what I seem."

He squinted and looked at me sideways. "Elaborate."

I swallowed again. "Look, I know what men think when they look at me. I know they see all my curves, beauty everywhere, and the devil-may-care look in my eyes. Those things should mean something… but they don't."

Fletch leaned on his elbow. "What should they mean?"

"They should mean that I'm a really good lay. That a woman who looks like me should be great in bed. She should be awesome, a sexual fantasy, the best--"

"But that's not true?" Fletch interrupted.

I shook my head slowly, no air left in my lungs. I had one hideous moment where I regretted having said that to Fletch. I should never have told him. I should have moved to Kansas and let a tornado take me away rather than explain to the one man I liked what was wrong. I turned to leave when his hand slid across mine. I looked back at him, but he didn't look horrified. He looked calm and like the news didn't scare him.

"It's okay," he said. "What if you went back to the beginning and told me what happened?"

Slowly, I moved back to my original position and opened my mouth to talk, but nothing came out. I cleared my throat and tried again. I couldn't bear to be specific, so I decided to be general. "It was a surprise to me too."

"What happened?" he asked softly.

"I haven't tried it that many times because it goes so badly. The first time was with my high school boyfriend after graduation. We'd been dating for over a year. I thought we'd get married. He'd waited because my family doesn't believe that kids should be having sex, so we'd waited until we were eighteen and graduated from high school. I thought he loved me. I thought he loved me more than anything. From the first moment, I screamed. I was not prepared for it to hurt like that. He didn't try for very long before he jumped up, put his clothes back on, said some incredibly hurtful things that he never took back, and left."

Fletch stroked my hand with his fingers. "It scared him off?"

"I saw him around that summer before he left for college. Little glimpses across malls and restaurants. We never spoke. He was supposed to go to college nearby, but after that, he moved to a different city. He didn't even say goodbye. I can't even think of how embarrassed the whole thing must have made him."

"Was the backlash from the breakup hard for you?"

I nodded. "I never told anyone what happened because I didn't want the news to circle back to him and add to his humiliation. I thought that, at least, I could give that to him. You know, since I loved him so much."

It was so quiet in the apartment, I felt like the only thing I could hear was the sound of my lips smacking as I spoke. Not even the sounds of my words were as loud as the smacking of my lips.

"Did you see a doctor?"

"No. I had bled like virgins are supposed to. I thought that boy had done the important bit and I hoped my next experience would be better."

"It wasn't?"

"If anything, it was worse. I was twenty-one and I'd been dating him for five months, he was getting impatient, and so was I. I really wanted my life to start, and everyone talks about how sex is the best thing all the time. I clenched my jaw and didn't scream, but it still hurt so bad, I can't explain. It hurt so bad I couldn't stop myself from crying. He noticed. Go up, told me he wasn't a rapist and was so embarrassed that he too walked out."

"Just for that?"

"He tried harder than Mr.-Teenage-Boyfriend, but he wasn't invested in me. The girl he left me for was nothing compared to me. She was dumpy, she laughed at stupid things, she applied her lipstick wrong, and the message I got is that sexual satisfaction is more important than looks, intelligence, or class. It trumped everything. I did go see a doctor, and he thinks he got my problem worked out. But he told me when I left his office that he might not have taken care of it completely and the only way for me to test it was to have sex. Except, I had no partner and I wasn't sure if I could have one. What if it went as badly as it had the first two times?"

"It's been a while since then, eh?"

"Yeah, it has been. And I'm tired. So tired," I admitted, leaning back. "I haven't felt like I could trust any of the men I've dated since then. Sure, they go off in raptures about how beautiful I am but I know that it isn't going to matter how beautiful I am if I can't give them a good time. I've been trying to find someone I could feel safe with. Someone who wouldn't get scared off by my imperfection."

His expression was thoughtful. "You still don't think that person is me, do you?"

I dropped one of my shoulders. "I think it could be. Otherwise, I would have left already."

He nodded. "Good. Your experience is so interesting because I've had the opposite experience."

"What do you mean?"

"I'm a terrific lay. I'm the best they've ever had, but they don't stay. They want someone with money, power, a respectable place to live, a serious job, and not just honorariums. I'm an artist and they want to lick chocolate sauce off my abs and come here when life treats them unkindly, but they don't want to be my wife. Live life side by side? Live life with me? I've asked women to live with me before as a stepping stone toward marriage, but the second they hear the word marriage, they freak out. You can see the panic rising behind their eyes. They don't want to marry me. They want to fool around with me… sometimes after they've already married someone else." He put up a hand. "I don't put up with that. I hope that explains why I thought I had the right to be so annoyed at you over Simon. I thought you should have told him sooner if you weren't interested. I didn't know he'd never asked if he could hold your hand."

I paused, looked at him, and asked quietly, "You want to get married?"

"I don't want to be single all my life," he replied.

"No… I mean. Do you want to marry me?" I whispered, but he heard me.

"What are you saying?"

I couldn't be more embarrassed than I already was. I might as well tell him the heart of what I wanted. "Look, after what has happened to me, what I really want is to get married. What I want is to get married, and instead of having an embarrassing evening together where I feel stripped, stupid, unloved, and unloveable, I have a honeymoon, where my new husband takes his time. And if the doctor didn't do a good enough job, my new husband will patiently wait for me…" I started tearing up. "And not be angry with me if things don't go so well at first. The doctor said I should be able to have a normal sex life, it just probably won't be amazing immediately."

Fletch put both his hands on mine, but I didn't dare look up into his face.

I had more to say. "But I don't want you to think that I am asking this because I think you would treat me right. Well, I do, but I love you. I love you and your little triangle, and your apartment that has no privacy, and the way you look at me when I suggest something crazy… and the sound of your voice, and the sight of your neck, and you have the most amazing--"

He kissed me.

"Of course, I'll marry you," he said when the kiss was over.

I nodded, clutching his hands. "Let's get married soon."

He put his forehead to mine. "Really soon."

Chapter Twenty Eight
The Wedding Invitation

Shannon and Fletch

Fletcher Litman and Shannon Bilx are pleased to announce their upcoming marriage on April the 14th, 20xx, at 4:00 p.m. at the Norcross Chapel on 97th and 104th Street. You are invited to attend, provided you can make it to the church on time.

Instructions and registration details are included on the back.

Dear Friends,

In planning our wedding, we decided to do what would make us the happiest. Planning a wedding for a year and spending $30,000 on our wedding would not make us happy. Instead, we have decided to get married in three weeks and we have decided to spend $3,000 on it. Some of you will be unhappy to learn that we have already spent most of that budget on Shannon's gown. When you see her on her wedding day, you will become happy again.

We require no wedding gifts as we are adults. We have ordered food, but it is only sandwiches and veggie platters. If you have any concerns about what might be in those sandwiches, we invite you to bring your own food. We welcome vegans, paleo, keto, and any other dietary restriction you might be on. Please don't be shy. This will be a child-friendly event and no alcohol will be served since the dinner will also be held in the church.

To answer some of the questions you may have:

We have been dating for two and a half months.

We are wildly, stupidly in love and appreciate that some of you will not approve of this whirlwind marriage. We are not interested in your words of caution. Please keep them to yourself… or at least, voice them where we can't hear you.

If you would like to merely pop in for the ceremony and leave during the dinner, we are fine with that.

We plan to move into Fletch's apartment.

Shannon's going to take his last name. Everyone needs to know she's not single anymore.

We are going on a honeymoon to Niagara Falls.

We did commission a wedding cake.

And we are wildly in love.

You may throw flower petals at us. Chase has volunteered to sweep them up after the ceremony.

Love,
Shannon and Fletch

Chapter Twenty Nine
Pre-Wedding Weather

Shannon

When I told Levi I needed two weeks off work, he said no.

"You don't have to pay me. I'm not taking vacation days or sick days. I'm taking two weeks off to get married," I said, trying to keep my temper from flaring.

"And I said I can't spare you," he replied hoarsely.

"Okay. In that case, next Friday will be my last day."

"What?" he growled. "That's a whole week before your wedding!"

"I know, but if you're going to back me into a corner and make me quit, then I may as well spend that last week getting ready. I already gave notice that I'll be moving out of my apartment, but I don't owe you a month's notice. Two weeks is good enough." I paused, seeing the upset on his face. "I don't like to do this to you, but you're being unreasonable. You know that, right?

"Shannon," he said, getting up from his desk and coming to talk to me at the door. "I was really nice when you called the other day and said you couldn't come in because of the ink. There's still some on your neck. Can't you call off your honeymoon and go later?"

"No. I can't," I said with a hand on my hip.

"Well, I can't find someone to replace you with only two weeks," he continued.

"You could find someone to replace me in five minutes if you called a temp agency. The work I do here isn't complex. Anyone could handle it."

Levi continued his awkward begging and it was so unlike him that I suddenly realized that something had changed. Carver and Levi knew each other and maybe Carver had promised him something in exchange for making himself a thorn in my side. If Levi did whatever Carver wanted, if I stayed working at the studio, I'd never get away from him.

"Listen," I said, thinking of all the time I'd worked for Levi. "My last day will be next Friday. Carver is the one who caused that ink incident. So far, the police haven't done anything about that, but I cannot continue to work for you if you continue to work with him. My problem isn't with you. It's with him."

Levi's hands were tied. He couldn't promise he wouldn't work with Carver. If Carver got a few of his bands to record their albums at his studio and word got out, that would be Levi's bread and butter. If Levi was the type of guy who'd play ball with Carver, maybe I didn't matter so much. There had to be plenty of innocent women to torture.

"You should start interviewing as soon as possible. I'll even help you find someone, but I can't stay whether I'm getting married or not."

"You're overreacting about the ink. It was just a joke," Levi said.

I picked up my feet and marched back to the front desk to get away from Levi, but he followed me. He was saying things like, "Why don't you like him? Couldn't you pull a practical joke on him as retribution? I'll buy the ink."

I was about to drive the heel of my shoe into the toe of his when I saw Natalie standing in the foyer. She was wearing heels made of leopard-print calf fur, skinny black leggings, a fur coat, and lime-colored glasses. I wasn't sure if I'd ever seen anyone try harder to look like a successful singer.

"Welcome to Music and Spirits," I said like I'd never seen her before. "How can we help you achieve your musical dreams today?"

"Shannon, it's me," she said, pulling off her sunglasses. "I bet you didn't recognize me!"

"I sure didn't. Look what the cat dragged in. How was your tour?"

"It was smashing!" She proceeded to lean against the counter of my desk like it was a bar and tell me and Levi all about her time on the tour bus.

She didn't know she was being unspeakably boring. The music industry had been losing appeal to me for some time, but when Natalie started talking about how the double-decker bus had beds on the top deck, I realized the last nail had been driven in the coffin. Whatever I did, wherever I went, I didn't want anything to do with the music industry.

I listened politely and tried to quietly get on with my work while she talked.

***

That night, I was having dinner with Fletch in a pita joint by city hall.

"I got offered the part in the play," he announced. "They don't start rehearsal until after we get back from Niagara Falls, so I thought it would be alright to accept."

I nodded. "Just out of curiosity, do you get paid?"

"This had better not be a deal-breaker. I get an honorarium. Probably three hundred bucks. At least, they don't charge me for the opportunity of doing it."

"It's not a deal-breaker. I just had to quit my job today."

He exhaled heavily. "Oh… that's a relief. I was wondering how I was going to tell you that you should really quit your job. What do you want to do instead?"

I paused. "I don't know. I'm not sure if anyone has ever asked me that. I'm good at books and paperwork and I don't mind passing my time that way. I always had to provide for myself, so I had to make money."

"What do you think about going to school for graphic design?" he suddenly asked.

I stuttered a laugh. "I can't do that. I've been living in a shoebox and I have been trying to save money, but my sisters take me shopping almost every week. It's shameful to admit, but I buy things. I can't afford to go to school."

"For just one second, don't think about the money. If you could do whatever you wanted to, what would it be?"

I hesitated. "I hate it and I love it when you see through me. Of course, I'd want to study graphic design, photography, all that stuff."

He wiped his mouth with a paper napkin. "What if I told you that I have a master's degree in music?"

I sipped on my drink. "What? The wild man with the abs and the mad drumming skills is a scholar?"

"I know I don't look the part with my shabby apartment and a different schedule every week. I had scholarships, and what I couldn't pay for out-of-pocket, my parents paid. I live in the apartment I have not because I'm broke, but because it's extremely convenient to be that close to the theater. Why do you think I gave Natalie seven hundred dollars for a mere chance to talk to you?"

"Because you're crazy? Money comes fast and goes even faster?" I balked, a little red-faced.

"No. Because seven hundred dollars isn't a big deal to me. Even if I put that money in my account, I wouldn't have spent it. Everything I do makes money, instead of swallowing it. I can't even think what I could spend seven hundred dollars on except you. If you want to go to school, I'll pay for it."

"Wait," I said, sending words to sneak up on him. "Didn't you say earlier that you don't have money, or power, or any of those things the other women want?"

"I'm not that man and I didn't offer you any of the things those women want. I didn't offer to get you your dream job. I didn't offer to buy you a huge house in the suburbs or a fancy car. I don't want to move. Where I live is exactly where I want to be, close to the theaters and where I want to work. I'm doing exactly what I want to do with my life and I want to offer you the same thing. The woman I know wants everyone to see her art and know she was here… and alive."

My heart was racing and a moment later I was crying. He came across to my side of the booth and slid in next to me. We kissed, and kissed, and kissed.

Had I never been seen by anyone before? Had no one in my whole life known me? Known who I was? Had I gone through this much of my life without being seen?

I held him tightly and wished that the moment would never end.

Chapter Thirty
Sisters of the Beast

Fletch

Shannon eyed me, looking me up and down. She bit her lip and shook her head. Finally, she said, "You can't wear that. A white shirt and black pants? Please? My sisters will eat you."

"I was going to wear a jacket over the shirt," I said, defending myself. "You'll like it better once I get the suit coat over top."

"No. I won't," she retorted. "You look hot. The coat probably makes you look even hotter. I bet the tailoring in the back makes your hips and back look smoldering, but I really don't know how my family will react to you, and those colors are fated to murder us. I feel like ink pranks are in the air. They'll ruin your shirt in one way and your pants in a completely different way."

She was wearing a turtleneck because she didn't want anyone to see the remaining smudges of ink that we hadn't been able to get off her neck yet. She'd paired it with blue jeans and boots.

"I'll just go through your closet," she offered. "It will be faster."

"I don't have a closet," I said as I chased her up the stairs and back into my apartment.

I spotted her going through my boxes. "Blue jeans. That will work best for the bottoms. And as for the top… why do I want to find you something printed? Do you have a shirt with a print?"

"The clothes you're recommending for me sound like they'll get ruined by an ink prank just as easily as what you're saying I can't wear," I reminded her as I reached for the top button on my pants.

She backed off and her face went very red. "Sorry. You look fine just the way you are. Where's your coat?"

"In my car," I replied as I refolded the clothes she'd pulled out of my dresser.

I smiled at her.

Her mother was making dinner for us at her family home out in the suburbs. I didn't know what to expect, but I imagined something like my parents' home. I hadn't been brought home to meet the family very often. Usually, the woman I was dating ran into her parents when she was with me. We'd be leaving the movie theater and they'd be there too and that's how we'd meet. She'd fluster her way through an introduction because she'd had no intention of ever introducing me to them. No Sunday dinner for me. But Shannon was bringing me home for Sunday dinner.

I felt a little like squealing.

On the drive over, Shannon was agitated and kept moving her hands and talking quickly. "I told you about my family, right? Who knows what terrible surprises they'll have waiting for us?"

"They know we're getting married, right?"

"Of course they know. I took my sisters to buy my wedding dress with me, not you. They asked me a million questions about you and I did my best not to give them any answers."

"What kind of questions?"

"Your shoe size. Your exact height. Your waist measurement. Sage thinks I couldn't be in love with you if I don't know your waist measurement." Shannon took a few quick inhales. "Don't open any doors when you're at my parents' house. The only time you can open a door is if you're leaving a bathroom. Otherwise, knock on the door until someone answers it. Don't move a partially open door either. Just don't touch any of the doors!"

"What? You think they'd prop a bucket of water over a door and let me get splashed? That seems pretty juvenile."

"And what? I'm a mastermind, crouching in corners and spray painting brick walls? We're excessively juvenile. They could fill a hallway with cups of water and make us empty them in order to get to the dinner table."

"Couldn't we just find another door?"

"Nope. There would be a prank at every door and every window. I don't think they'd splash us with water, but they would definitely splash us with glitter, which might be worse. There is glitter in my parents' couch from ten years ago. My mother won't get a new couch because what would be the point? It would get some other unspeakable thing on it in no time."

"Do any of your siblings still live at home?"

"No, but the grandkids come over now and they're worse than their parents," she sighed.

"Tell me about your sisters. I want to guess their names when I see them," I coaxed.

"My oldest sister's name is Tallis. She's married and has two kids. Hers are the ones most often at my parents' house because she still works part-time and my mom looks after them while she's at work. Then there's Sage. She's married, but no kids yet. Then there's my brother, Ethan. Honestly, we forgot he existed after he married Tiffany. She's just like us. She fits in so well with my family, I don't know if she even remembers she isn't my mother's daughter. Then there's me, and my little sister, Quinn."

"Why is this the first time I'm even hearing these names?"

"They're monsters. If I didn't love my mother, I would have begged you to elope with me, but I know she wants to see me get married. She's not fussy or anything, and she's already told me she has no problem with our wedding plans. She just wants to see me get married and she's so satisfied with my dress it's ridiculous. She's going to hire a team of photographers to make sure they get amazing pictures of me."

"And me?"

"No, Fletch, they're going to leave you out of the shots. We're the type of people who don't care about the groom. It's all about the girls and their day."

"Which is the only sensible thing," I added.

"Okay… we're here."

There were hand signals and muttering on the other side of the vehicle as we pulled up.

"Did you just cross yourself?" I asked her. "I didn't know you were Catholic. We're getting married in a reformation church."

"I'm not Catholic. I've never crossed myself before. I'm just praying that they didn't unload all the neighbors' garbage across the front lawn and dress Tallis up like the Trash Heap from *Fraggle Rock*."

"Your family sounds awesome," I said as I unbuckled my seatbelt.

She cautiously got out of the car and looked around like she was expecting someone to jump out at her. "The porch light is off. None of the house lights are on either. It looks like they're going to pretend like no one is home." She glanced over at me. "Juvenile enough for you?"

I pulled my jacket out of the backseat and put it on.

No one jumped out at us as we made our way across the driveway and up the front steps. She rang the doorbell.

"Should we just go in?" I asked her when no one answered. I put my hand on the doorknob and she slapped it away.

"You're acting like an amateur, Fletch. What was the first thing I told you? Don't open a door. I haven't brought a boyfriend home since the guy *before* Mr.-Teenage-Romance. Me bringing a man home at all would be weird, but me bringing my fiance is something completely different. I can't even imagine what zany tricks they have up their sleeves. When Sage brought Richard home, they accidentally set him on fire."

"You're only telling me this now?"

She shrugged her shoulders. "It was an accident with sparklers. I didn't even know you *could* set someone on fire with sparklers."

"If you don't want him to be set on fire then keep him on the step," we heard a voice call out from behind the bushes.

A second later, a firework went off. It was a big pink one, like a ball that leaped into the air and then fizzled. Then the music started. It was *Eternal Flame* by the Bangles. Her family was in a line in the yard. Someone in the back was setting off Roman candles, big pink ones, and beautiful ones that glittered and the music rang out. They were singing along with the music.

I reached for Shannon and she reached for me.

We watched as the sparklers and the fireworks lit up the night sky. If it was cold that night, I couldn't remember that it was. The only thing I remembered was how happy Shannon's family was for her, and how the only practical joke was a whoopee cushion that one of the grandkids put on her chair.

Chapter Thirty One
Wedding Day

Shannon

I stayed over at my parents' house the night before the wedding. All the girls stayed with me, and though there were many jokes, most of them were merely in the form of unusual lingerie. When I woke up, I immediately went to make sure no one had written on my face that night. No one had, which was good, because I had had it with ink pranks.

After breakfast, Quinn took charge of getting me ready. She was the youngest and knew more about current trends in hair and makeup than I did. We didn't even talk about how she was going to do my hair beforehand.

She made me sit on a chair and narrowed her eyes. "Romantic or edgy?"

"What does that really mean, Quinn?"

Sage came up behind her. "If you choose romantic, it will be a symmetrical hairstyle. Probably right down the back. If you choose edgy, it'll be a side thing."

"Oh, the side thing. My dress isn't symmetrical, so go look at it, and decide which side to make bigger."

After inspecting it, she decided to do a curled bun behind my right ear.

The day was pleasant as we had lunch as a family, and I got hauled away for a manicure afterward.

My mother got out her camera and took me to the backyard to get a headstart on the pictures, taking cutesy pictures with each of my sisters and my sister-in-law. Sage took the camera away from her when the photographer arrived and took more with me and my parents.

"We should have had Fletch come over," she complained. "That old tradition about the groom not seeing the bride before the wedding is so old-fashioned. He should be here with us, getting a headstart on being part of the family."

My breath caught.

I think it was at that moment that I knew he wasn't going to make it to the ceremony.

***

I pushed the thought away at first, but once we were all packed into the car on the way to the church, I got out my cell phone and tried calling him. No answer. Frustrated and cross, I dialed Simon's number.

"Hi, Simon, is Fletch around?"

"You mean, he's not with you?" Simon said on the other end of the line.

"No."

"He was here at his parents' house until last night. He wasn't in bed when we got up this morning and we thought he'd snuck off to spend the night with you."

"He didn't do that. I haven't seen him. He hasn't called me either." I felt a chill crawl up my spine under my satin dress and suddenly the chill went hot. "Do you have any idea where he might have gone?"

Simon sounded worried on the other end. "He might have gone home."

"Simon," I said sternly. "I need you and anyone else who's free to find him. Go to his apartment. Call Chase if you know him, or go to the Eloquent Spider. Go to the music shop, the theater, and anywhere prominent where he's played. I'll go to the church and see if he's there, but I feel sick like something terrible has happened. Him not answering his phone on our wedding day is a prank he wouldn't pull."

"It's okay, Shannon. I'm sure he's doing an errand that makes perfect sense, like buying you a ring. It's so weird that you two didn't get an engagement ring or wedding rings. He probably realized it's nuts not to have one and went ring shopping."

"He would have picked up his phone if he were doing something like that."

"Maybe not. Maybe he wanted it to be a surprise."

"I hope so," I said, gazing out the window. "We're at the church. I'll check it out and call you back if he's here."

"Great," Simon said as he hung up.

***

That was the story of how I got jilted on my wedding day. It was a masterful prank. I gave up waiting in the back of the church and stood at the doors where the guests were coming in. I was there because I wanted to see Fletch as soon as he came in. Everyone was in such high spirits when they arrived, only to see me and have their faces fall. The groom seeing the bride before the wedding was one thing, but the guests seeing her before the wedding was something else entirely. All of them knew something was wrong as soon as they saw me.

It was an event intended to humiliate me.

Eventually, Simon came through the doors panting and out of breath with the other boys. "We couldn't find him. I guess he's not here either."

I shook my head.

At the very least, I had neither started crying nor allowed my face to show the rage that was seething behind my mask of perfect calm. Half an hour had passed since the wedding should have begun.

I turned to Tallis, who was at my elbow. "Wanna do something you've never done before?" I said to her.

"Yup," she replied.

"Go in there and tell them that the groom has gone missing, but everyone is welcome to the food in the hall of the church. Reassure everyone that we're still expecting him to show and when he gets here, we'll still have a wedding."

"Wait. If we've got to that point, do you really have no idea where he is?"

"My guess as to what has happened is pretty terrifying."

"What do you mean?"

"I mean that I don't think there's the tiniest chance that Fletch jilted me on our wedding day on purpose. I think he was kidnapped."

Tallis dropped a shoulder. "That sounds crazy."

"Does it?" I hissed. "Some pretty crazy things have been going on lately. You know what I need?"

"What?"

"I need a gun, a set of handcuffs, and a car."

She laughed. "You've lost your mind. What kind of stuff have *you* been up to that you're even talking like that?"

"Look, I didn't want to scare anyone with the crazy scenarios that have been playing out lately, and now isn't the time to talk about them. Get in there and make that announcement," I said, giving her a push.

She held back. "If you had that stuff, do you think you could get him?"

"I don't know if all that is necessary. I think the point of all this is to ruin my wedding, make a fool of me, and, if possible, make it so that I can't marry Fletch."

"If it's any consolation, you don't look humiliated, even though getting jilted on your wedding day is pretty much the pinnacle of humiliation."

"I'm more sad than anything. All those people feel sorry for me."

"Anything you've ever wanted to do in front of a crowd?" Tallis suddenly asked, turning the question I'd asked her around on me.

I laughed.

"It might give him some more time to get here."

Chapter Thirty Two
Six Hours Earlier

Fletch

I didn't have that much experience with tranquilizers. Even though I couldn't move my limbs or open my eyes, I knew that was what had been used on me. More than being afraid that I had been kidnapped, I was pissed off. No matter what urgency I felt inside as my body bumped in the backseat of a car, I couldn't move to stop what was happening. I could hear voices, but I couldn't identify them.

Soon, I stopped hearing the conspiring voices, stopping feeling the humming rhythm of the vehicle and stopped sensing anything at all.

My sight was foggy and fuzzy as I awoke.

Morning sunlight blistered through my eyelids. I breathed and coughed. As I opened my eyes, I saw things that didn't make sense. The ceiling was yellow. No one painted ceilings yellow. Not even my mad mother. I saw a kitchen cabinet even though I was lying on a bed. I saw a steering wheel.

Then suddenly, I realized that I had never been in a car.

I tried to sit up but unsuccessful, I fell back down. I was in a camper, and someone was in the bed with me. A foot hit my leg.

I turned to see who it was. I couldn't see their face, but I saw the hair so purple it could only belong to Ringlet. I didn't want to call her Rin anymore, not after what she'd helped Carver do at the last concert, but using all seven letters of her name instead of three seemed like paying her too much respect.

Managing to get to my feet, I bumped my way down the corridor of the camper to the driver's seat. From that vantage point, all I could see were rolling hills and sky. No people and no buildings in sight. We were nowhere, but the keys were in the ignition. When I tried them, the engine turned over, but only once. Looking at the dials, it was easy to see what was wrong. The camper was out of gas.

I left it and went back to Rin. I tapped her with my shoeless foot. "Wake up," I ordered loudly.

She rolled over and pretended to be as drugged and groggy as I was, but I knew it was an act.

I prodded her again. "Look, whatever you're going to say you did to land yourself in this situation, I already know it's a lie. Carver added that mini fruit pizza to our order and paid the pizza boy to deliver it saying it was a promotional item. My boys didn't eat it because I was the one getting married today, so they left it for me. I felt tired and went to bed early. You and Carver snuck into the house and pulled me out of bed, and I was too out of it to do anything about it. You managed to get me in this camper. He left and you drove around until you ran out of gas, and now you're pretending that you were drugged too, when, actually, you're fine. You're just here to make sure I stay here for the rest of the day and miss my wedding."

"You're wrong. I'm as much of a victim as you are," she said drowsily.

In a rage, I grabbed the mattress and pulled it out from under her. "Don't act like you're drugged!"

She fell on her butt and righted herself as quickly as a cat. "Okay, fine," she panted from the corner of the camper. "I'm not drugged, but that doesn't mean I'm not cornered. Carver said he'd cancel Blades and Blasters' contract if I didn't help him. I can't lose that contract."

"And we're just supposed to stay here for the day?" I asked, tossing the foam mattress next to her.

"Yeah," she affirmed, putting the mattress back in place.

"You don't have a phone?"

"Carver will get us at midnight," she replied, still rattled.

I looked down at my feet. I wasn't even wearing shoes. They were trying to make it so I couldn't even walk out.

She got up and opened the minifridge. "He's not trying to torture you. There's enough food here to last until he comes to get us. I'm here to keep you company and entertain you."

The sound that came out of my mouth was almost the same as the one a drunk makes when they're vomiting in the bathroom. "Entertain me? Like you could."

She huffed. "I'm sure I could entertain you. After all, I'm an entertainer."

I ground my teeth together. "If you try to sing to me, I swear, I'll break something. Maybe everything."

"Well, you don't have to take it out on me. I am here, but I didn't do this to you. It wasn't my idea," she justified as she covered her tank top with a plaid shirt.

"I can't think of a single reason not to take it out on you," I said frostily. "Have you ever wanted to marry someone?"

She looked at me like she couldn't believe that anyone was that stupid. That anyone was stupid enough to believe in marriage.

"You haven't, huh?"

With those words, she was reduced to a little girl who hadn't properly plunged the depths of human emotion. That wouldn't bother most people, but Rin was a songwriter, and even hinting at her being immature made her insane.

She opened her mouth, but I cut her off. "If you start singing, I'll rip the fridge out of the wall. You're here to be my punching bag. What did you think was going to happen? I was going to think this was a sweet little waiting room? You'd feed me grapes, sing to me, and I'd be so blown away by your talent that I wouldn't mind missing my wedding?"

Rin averted her eyes.

"Argh!" I balled my fists together and instead of punching anything, I merely held them at my temples while I screamed. Then I dropped my hands. "You know what, Rin? Do you know what I wanted for my life? I wanted music, just like you, but not as much as you. I wanted to have someone in the audience who was just for me. Fans? It's nice when people appreciate your music. That leaves a good feeling, but it wasn't the same as having *her* in my audience. I have never wanted another person's approval so much in my life. That first night, I was playing the triangle, but she told me it sounded like a baby star being born. I have been hooked, addicted, and completely hers since I met her. And you and Carver put all those gross inky words all over her. I never want to see you again. How could this be friendly? How could I think anything good about you again? How will I sit through a car ride back to the city without killing Carver? My wedding wasn't supposed to be a big event. I wasn't doing it for attention. I just wanted to tie her to me in a way so that everyone understands how much I adore her, that I would do anything for her, even let myself be tied down." I kicked the fridge and sat back on the bed in a huff.

"Fletch," she said quietly. "You should forget all about Shannon. Even if you marry her, you'll never shake Carver. For whatever reason, he's just as obsessed with her as you are, except he's not normal. He doesn't understand boundaries and I don't know if he'll ever leave her alone."

I shook my head. "I don't care what he wants. What size are your shoes?"

"There's no way you can wear my shoes. They're size seven."

"What's that in mens'?"

"It's a five and a half," she answered coldly.

I gnawed on the side of my cheek. "That's not going to work."

Thinking, I opened the door to the camper and felt the wind in the spring air. If I didn't get a lot more clothes, a walk anywhere was going to be out of the question. I closed the door and went back to the driver's seat. I couldn't see any road signs.

"Where are we?" I yelled to Rin.

"I'm not supposed to tell you."

"How is Carver going to find us?"

"He told me where to drive. He'll drive the way he told me and pick us up at midnight. I already told you."

I looked out at the pavement. We were on a side road. Someone might drive by. I turned on the emergency lights. If someone drove by I'd flag them down. Ringlet pouted in the back while I kept my eyes on the road and the side view mirror.

"I'm cold," I called back to her. "I saw you put on another shirt. Is there anything else for me to wear?"

She threw me the blanket that had been on the bed. I put it over my knees and kept watching.

Chapter Thirty Three
Fast Forward to the Wedding

Shannon

I looked at Tallis. Was there anything I ever wanted to do in front of a crowd? I suddenly realized that there was.

I stepped past her and walked down the aisle even though there was no groom to greet me. Once there, I turned and spoke to our guests. "Hello, everyone!" I said brightly. "I'd like to welcome all of you to my wedding. Naturally, Fletch is supposed to be here to marry me and many of you have noticed that he's not. The thing is… I don't think he's standing me up on our wedding day. I think he's been genuinely held up. His phone is not working. So, instead of having the wedding first, I thought it would be okay if we gave him a little more time to get here and just reorganized our events. The food has already been set out, so if you'd all like to head into the hall, we'll have dinner."

As soon as people started standing up, Fletch's mother rushed me. "What do you mean, he's not here?"

I met her gaze steadily. "I'm not hiding him. I don't know where he is. The only thing I know is that he would not have deserted me if he could help it. We have to hang on."

She straightened herself. "What can I do to help?"

"You can get that look off your face. Until they kick us out of the church at midnight, this is still my wedding day, and if you can smile and have a good time, that would really help out.

Don't even look tense. Everything is going to work out just fine. Have faith in your son."

A strange look crossed my soon-to-be mother-in-law's face. "And you're sure he hasn't walked out on you?"

I stood firm. "Fletch would not do that. If he wanted to dump me, he would have told me to my face. He would have told you. He would not allow his family and friends to be inconvenienced at a non-existent wedding all night. If he wanted to dump me he would have no interest in humiliating me."

My faith in him moved her. Her face changed. "I suppose all that is true," she said softly. "I made a mistake just now when I asked you that. Of course, he would have told us."

I nodded at her and sent her to join her husband.

My family was waiting in the wings, flocking toward me as soon as Fletch's mother had gone. "What can we do?"

I grabbed my brother Ethan by the arm. "Make sure the microphone system in the hall works. I'm going to make an announcement later."

"No problem," he said as he left.

"What about the rest of us?"

I cracked my neck. "Go pretend to have a good time and if anyone asks anything, just say I said it all when I spoke up. Don't cut the cake yet."

Most of them left, but my mom hung back. "Do you think he'll make it?"

"I don't know if he will," I replied. "There is someone really nasty out there who wants to get my attention this way. I can't believe they would stoop this low. My instinct is to chase after him and find out what he has done with Fletch, but tonight, I

have the frustrating job of staying still. He'll come here and I
have to be here when he gets here."

"Who is trying to ruin your wedding?"

"Carver Criche."

"He's here," my mother said. "He signed the guestbook."

Chapter Thirty Four
Gang it all!

Fletch

I saw a pack of motorcycles coming down the road. I palmed the horn, rolled down the window, and waved at them.

Rin came running. "What are you calling them for?"

"I need a ride to my wedding," I explained tersely.

"Yeah, but you don't need help from them. Don't you know who they are?" she screamed as she pulled my hand off the horn. "They're Hell's Dragons. It's one of the biggest gangs around these parts. We do not want them messing with us."

"I just want a ride. Maybe they can help me get back to town, or better still, away from you and away from Carver. I would, dead serious, rather ride with them than with him."

Her lower lip quivered in anger. "No. You don't know them. You don't know what they're like. You can't go with them. You won't be safe."

I continued waving and honked the horn again. "You think I'm safe with you?"

Her eyes widened.

The bikers pulled up and Rin disappeared into the back of the camper.

One of them stopped next to me and raised his visor. "What's up?"

"We're out of gas and I am going to miss my wedding if I don't get back to the city. Could I get a ride?"

The biker moved his tongue around his teeth like that was the way decisions were made. "I'd need to talk to the guys."

I inclined my hand politely. "Please do."

Rin returned from the back with a red gas can. She hopped out of the trailer and circled to the tank. "That won't be necessary," she said in an overly cheery tone. "I was just tricking him. We aren't really stranded."

The biker looked at her with drooping eyelids. "Are you the bride?"

"No," she said as she opened the gas cap.

"Is she the stripper from your bachelor party?"

"No. She's a kidnapper! Would you believe it?" I said, feeling the tension escape from my shoulders.

He stroked his beard and peered at her, his disgust evident. "If that isn't the worst trick to play on someone, keeping a man from his wedding? Do you know how many years a man waits to get married?"

She put her hands on her hips and tried to smile. "I've been told."

"Do you want us to take her with us so you can drive straight there?" the biker offered.

My eyebrows went up. I was sorely tempted.

"You wouldn't!" she cried as she lifted the can to fill the tank.

The biker waved a dismissing hand at her and turned back to me. "How far do you have to go? That's not a lot of gas."

"Edmonton."

He looked at it and then at the camper. "You might not make it. You got any money?"

"Do you have any money, Rin?" I called.

"Yup. Loads of money. There's so much of it, it's coming out of my ears."

The biker got out his wallet and gave me two twenty-dollar bills. "I hope this helps. Seriously, want us to take her with us? She'd look good on the wall."

I chuckled. "I think I have to return her to her owner. Thank you for the money."

"Think of it as a wedding present."

Rin replaced the gas cap and turned to the biker. "Everything is sorted now. You can go."

He regarded her with an emotion that was best friends with boredom, except lower on a mood spectrum. "I'll wait until I see him drive away."

She eyed the gangsters and rushed to get back in the camper.

"What's your name, friend?" I asked pleasantly.

"Santa."

"Are you sure it's not Mr. Claus?"

"I go by that too," he said with a smile.

"I'm Fletch," I volunteered. "And thank you again."

Rin got in the seat beside me.

Looking at her, a huge problem just struck me. I turned back to the biker. "Where are we? How do I get back to Edmonton?"

He grinned and told me the way.

Chapter Thirty Five
Five-Thirty at the Wedding

Shannon

"Aren't you going to eat anything?" my mother asked as I took a break from working the room.

"Nope. I'm just moving around to avoid Carver. He's over there trying to look like Humphrey Bogart in the fedora and failing. Did you see the look on his face? This is clearly not the wedding he envisioned for me."

"Why not?" my mom asked huffily. From the pictures I'd seen, her wedding was very similar to what Fletch and I had planned.

"He thinks I'm a badass, and this is entirely too wholesome."

She huffed again. "Why would he think that about my daughter?"

I smiled. "I'm about to explain it to everybody." We had been moseying along, greeting people on the way to talk to Ethan. I stopped to talk to anyone who looked at me.

They said things like, "You're holding up well!"

Like I wouldn't hold up well!

"You look so beautiful!"

I always looked beautiful.

I got to Ethan. "Have you got a microphone ready for me?"

"You're going to talk more?" he gawked. "No one likes listening to you talk."

"I know," I laughed like he had just given me a compliment. He was right though. He knew me well enough to know my insides did not match my outsides. My mouth was how my insides came out. But today was the day to let it all hang out. "Can I have the microphone, please? It's my day."

"You're always such a glutton for public humiliation. Should we get grandma out of the room?"

"Why would we bother with that? Someone will just tell her after the fact what I did or show her the evidence. Are the live streams ready?"

He groaned. "You are out of your mind."

Nevertheless, he handed me the microphone, got out of the way of the cameras, and I took it. "Is everybody having a good time?" I asked the crowd.

I got a few random cheers from the tables with my siblings at them.

I glanced at Ethan to make sure he was still live streaming it. When I got the thumbs up from him, I continued.

"Great. Normally, at this point in a wedding, we would have actually had a wedding and so it would be customary to toast the bride and the happy couple, but this is not a normal wedding. I want to tell you the story of how Fletch and I met. The thing is, I kidnapped him."

Only the fiddle player from Fletch's orchestra made a sound.

"I put a toy gun to his back and ordered him into a car. I bet some of you are wondering why I did that. It was a case of mistaken identity. I thought Fletch was someone else. I had a friend, who isn't here tonight, who wanted to get the attention of a certain man in the music industry. She asked for my help and as some of you know, I can't say no to a prank. Except this didn't turn out to be a very good one. Even though we successfully kidnapped Fletch and handcuffed him to a stove in a camp kitchen, he wasn't who we thought he was. We were trying to kidnap Carver Criche." Our eyes met across the hall.

His jaw clenched and he pulled his fedora further down his forehead, but he didn't leave his chair.

I went on. "My friend and I fought and she hit me over the head with a brick. I was unconscious and she panicked because she didn't know what to do. Fletch, however, had a cool head and had her bring me into the camp kitchen. Seeing me on the floor, he recognized me. He had never met me, but he knew who I was from the trail of broken hearts I left behind me. I'd hurt someone important to him and he didn't want to miss the opportunity to let me have it. When I woke up, I was handcuffed to him through the stove and I couldn't get away. So, he told me what he thought of me." I smiled at everyone. "I know, the romance is almost too much."

I got a couple of laughs at that, aside from the owl-like attention I got from every adult in the room.

"So, we fought about what I had done, who was wrong, and what a rat I was. At the end of the night, he said he wanted one more thing before he unlocked the cuffs. He told me he wanted to go on a date with me, just to see what I looked like when I ruined a man's life. I thought that sounded like great fun and agreed to go. Our first date was magical. I didn't have to pretend to be someone I wasn't. I could say what I really felt and thought."

I hadn't meant to cry, but I felt myself tearing up. "I don't know if any of you understand how it feels when you think that no one could love you, really love you, because your insides are filled with confetti crumbs labeled with your faults. I have always sought to be understood on a level that kept people as far away from me as possible. Communicate with others so they can never communicate back, but they would know I was here, that I thought things, and did things. Fletch changed all that because I could be me, and it was clear that he loved me anyway. Insecurities, fears, fake battle armor and all."

I started playing with the strap of my wedding gown. "Except, there was a problem. I was supposed to kidnap Carver Criche that night and he knew it. He was upset that I didn't kidnap him. He got a fake gun and came after me, wondering why I didn't do what I was supposed to. When he didn't get what he wanted, he came to my work. When that didn't work, he went after Fletch, and through other people, offered him a job that would take him far away from me. When that didn't work out, he broke into my apartment with a real gun and left me handcuffed to my bed."

"How did you get out?" someone from the back yelled. It might have been Carver himself who asked.

"Bolt cutters under the bed. I'm not twelve."

"Is that why you have bolt cutters under the bed? In case you get handcuffed to your bed?" someone else called.

I waved my hand airly at the accusation. "Actually, it isn't. The bolt cutters are for my art. I am an artist and I need proper cutters for thick wire and other hardware. You see, I'm so shy that my family doesn't even know about my art projects. I have felt the need to keep myself so hidden that no one even knows what food I like."

I smiled. That was some championship PR spinning.

"After the handcuffing thing, I received a dress in the mail that I thought was from Fletch, but wasn't." I turned around to see the picture Ethan had projected on the wall. The projector was meant for a slide show of the pictures I had taken of Fletch and me when we were on dates, but instead, it was one of the pictures Officer Todd had taken of me in the bathroom of the Eloquent Spider. It was the most pitiful one, where I had been crying and there were mascara smears down my face. The words 'I want Carver' were plainly seen across my chest, as well as the ink smear around my neck.

"This is a picture the police took of me that night," I said, looking straight at the spot Carver had been a moment ago. He was gone.

I peered over the crowd. Had he left the building completely?

I brought the microphone to my lips. "I don't think Fletch is missing out on our wedding because he wants to stand me up. I think he's been kidnapped to keep him from getting here. Isn't it amazing how a prank with an orange water pistol can elevate so quickly? In case some of you don't know, my little confession has been filmed and posted to every social media outlet that can support it. I want off this carousel." I looked directly into the camera. "Please repost and help my fiance make it to our wedding."

Chapter Thirty Six
Five-Thirty in the City

Fletch

I got gas, but forty dollars in that gas guzzler wasn't going to take us far.

Rin's cell phone had magically reappeared and she had been sending texts the whole drive back to the city. Whatever happened, she wanted to make sure her contract with Carver remained intact, so she was giving him everything she could. I would have let her drive to stop her from texting, but she would have turned the camper around and gone in the wrong direction.

"Since you had a gas can in the camper, I guess Carver was never going to come back to get us and that was another one of your lies. At midnight, you were going to fess up to the truth and drive us back to the city then?"

"Yup," she said with a pop of her lower lip while she stared at her phone.

"Does Carver have my wallet and keys?" I persisted.

"I don't really know," she said coldly.

From that, I had to assume that he did. In that case, I wasn't going to drive back to my parents' house. My place was on the way to the church, whereas my parents' place was out of the way. If I made it back to the fragrance store, the lady who ran it had a spare key to my apartment in case of an emergency. I just had to make it back before she locked up.

I pulled up in front of the shop. Sunlight glistened off the store front's glass panels and I wasn't sure if she was still in. I hopped out onto the sidewalk.

The door was locked. I cupped my hands around my eyes and peered inside. No one was there.

Rin got behind the wheel and skidded away.

I didn't care. If I had been worried about her leaving me in the lurch, I would have taken the camper keys with me the same way I had when I got gas. I was thrilled to be rid of her, but now I was on the sidewalk with no shoes, no coat, no phone, and no idea how to get into my apartment on the second floor.

The music store wasn't that far away, but it would also be closed.

I banged my fist against the wall and shouted.

A siren went off behind me. "Sir, you can't beat up buildings."

I turned around. A police cruiser had pulled up to the curb, and an officer had sprung from it. The siren had stopped, but the lights kept flashing. It was Officer Todd.

"I thought that was you," he said in a friendly way. "Aren't you supposed to be at your wedding?"

"I am," I replied, so relieved I couldn't explain it.

"Yeah, the guests at your wedding are going nuts. Shannon has been posting every five minutes asking if anyone has any idea where you are. You look like you could use a hand. You are aware you're still wearing your pajamas."

"I know. I came home to get a suit. I have ten of them, but I haven't got my house keys, and as much as I want to marry

Shannon, I don't want to go to my wedding in an undershirt and pajama pants."

Todd nodded. "Yeah. I can't get you into your apartment, but if you're not picky, I can get you something to wear."

"I'm not!" I declared.

"I can give you a ride to the church too!" he winked.

And I happily went with him.

Chapter Thirty Seven
Six O'Clock

Shannon

"Let's take down the tables and move the chairs to the edges of the room!" I said, still stalling. "We can still have music and dancing, and people can talk on the outskirts if they want."

"Shannon," my cousin Francene interrupted. "I know I said I wanted to dance at your wedding, but this isn't what I had in mind."

"No one had this in mind, Frankie. But I refuse to fall apart. I plan to keep this party going until midnight if I must."

"You should at least cut the cake," she complained.

Despite my best efforts, my shoulders fell a little as I sighed. "It may come to that. I may even send someone to do a chip run. I have no idea. People don't have to stay if they don't want to though. This is my fight."

"Oh no," she said quickly, shaking her head and hands in unison. "I'll stay."

"Really?"

"Whose wedding is like this? It's chaos."

I smiled and patted her arm. "I appreciate the support."

Fletch's boys were doing what I said and had begun taking down tables in the most leisurely manner. Just the way I liked it.

Ethan had turned on the speaker and was playing music both wholesome and nostalgic, which I also appreciated. It wasn't even loud, which was why I was so surprised when two police officers entered the hall.

They wore their hats pulled down over their eyes. Was the one in the back Officer Todd? I couldn't tell at that distance.

"We've had a noise complaint," the one in the front said loudly. "You'll have to turn the music down."

I had never heard such a crisp authoritative voice in my life. My spine went rigid and every single one of my wedding guests stopped what they were doing. The only sound that was made was the tinny music coming from Ethan's speaker. Eyes were wide. Mouths hung open. People whispered panicked words into the ear of the person next to them. Probably most of them had never been to a party the police broke up before. Some of them looked worried.

All this time, I'd only been dealing with Officer Todd and guys like him on the force. I'd never once come head-to-head with a real hardliner. Well, I could do it. I rolled my shoulders and approached him.

"Sorry about the noise," I said sweetly.

"No, seriously," he said, his jaw clenching and unclenching with his words. He pointed at me and the people around me. "You're going to have to turn that music off, round up all these wedding guests, and get them back into the chapel."

I stared at him. Something was off.

He continued, "Because the groom has arrived for the wedding." He swept his hat off and there was Fletch.

I leaped into his arms.

The crowd thawed.

"Wait, do you have the wedding license?" I asked in sudden fear. It would be terrible if I had kept all the guests here and we couldn't do the wedding after all because of a technicality.

Simon leaped forward. "I have it. I also have your vows."

As people hurried into the chapel, I held him back. "Isn't it illegal to wear a police officer's uniform because you aren't supposed to impersonate a cop?"

"Maybe," Fletch shrugged. "It was either this or my jam jams. I'll go to jail if I have to."

"You look terrific," I said as my sisters pulled me away. I kept my eyes on him for as long as possible, until I was swept around a corner.

"You look a complete mess," Quinn complained as she corrected my makeup. "I'm not even going to bother recurling your hair. We'll just pin in up."

"It doesn't even matter," I sang. "He made it!"

"You know," Tallis said thoughtfully as she leaned against the counter in the bathroom. "Was what you said true, Shannon?"

"What?"

"That you didn't think anyone could love you? Was that true?"

I nodded. "Before Fletch, the only time I ever really felt loved, it didn't work. He didn't really love me. When things didn't go his way, he bailed. I was a bit traumatized by the whole thing."

"But you know that we love you, right?"

I smiled for my sisters who did not pull a prank on Fletch when I brought him home that first night. They had been happy for me. "Of course, I know that," I smiled.

She put her hands on her hips. "As long as you know that much."

"Thank you, for being there for me," I said, and I meant it. She knew it.

Quinn finished touching me up and my sisters hurried out of the bathroom. I didn't have any bride's maids or flower girls, so my father met me outside the bathroom and led me down the aisle to Fletch, who for all the world looked like a stripper who hadn't gotten started yet. Simon and Officer Todd stood up with him.

My father raised my veil, kissed my cheek, and handed me off to Fletch with all the happiness of a proud father.

The minister spoke.

I was so ruffled I didn't hear what he said until he got to the part where we were supposed to talk. "Fletcher and Shannon have asked to read their own vows and then to make the traditional vows on top of them. Fletcher?"

He pulled a paper out of his pocket. It was a photocopy of the inside of a book. I recognized it.

"Wait," I said, showing him that I had done the exact same thing.

It was the thing that changed my life. It was the thing someone had written in the back of the book about the girl who fell down the well. I showed it to him on our second date.

Fletch smiled. "We'll read it together. Each a line until the end," he offered. "I'll start." Then he raised his voice, "I'm not important."

"I'm a few scratches of ink on a page," I said.

"I shouldn't even be here."

"But I am."

He read on, "As unlikely as it is."

"You're here reading me." My eyes got glassy.

"And I adore you for it."

"You've only been reading me for a few blinks of your eyes."

His jaw clenched for a second before he spoke the next words. "And if that's all we have."

"I'm grateful."

"Wouldn't it be something?"

"If our connection could be something more?" I said wistfully.

"If I could see you..." Fletch said.

"And you could see me," I said.

"If I could catch you when you fall."

"I could be your heart," I said, struggling to make my words clear.

"And you could be my soul," he said with conviction.

"Each day..."

"Forever..."

"I'd be yours," we said together.

We held hands across the space between us and put our foreheads together. No two people ever stood so close together as their minister finished their wedding ceremony.

We kissed, and I could feel how our love hit everyone. Everyone in the chapel could feel it because when I turned to see our friends and family, there wasn't a dry eye in the house.

We returned to the hall, had cake, and accepted the good wishes of our guests.

"I am sorry about one thing," I whispered to Fletch between well-wishers. "That you didn't see me in my wedding gown coming down the aisle the way you're supposed to."

"Yeah, it was pretty unfair of me to steal the show. No one is ever excited about the groom's entrance."

I smacked his arm playfully. "It's not about that. You can be the star of the show. I don't mind. I just wanted to see your face look all joyful with anticipation when I came into view. As it happened, when you saw me in my dress for the first time, I was quelling wedding guests, and your hat was covering your eyes."

"Hmmm," he said, pausing to shake someone's hand and accept their congratulations. When he finally turned back to me, he said, "Want me to buy you a different dress? We could have another ceremony and renew our vows?"

"Five seconds after our wedding?" I gasped.

"We could do this every year if you'd like. Have a bigger party each year to celebrate our anniversary. Imagine how many dresses you'd have by the end? No need to be bridezilla because there'd always be next year, like Christmas. Every year, you could make a grand entrance, and every year you could see the anticipation on my face for the moment when you come into view."

I looked skeptical. "But it won't be the *first* time, like tonight."

He returned my expression. "You might not know this, but the first time is not usually the best. Trust me, I'll be excited each and every time."

Officer Todd approached and said pleasantly to Fletch, "You can drop those clothes off at the station tomorrow."

"I surely can do that. Our honeymoon doesn't officially start until the day after tomorrow. Thank you so much for the ride and for coming to get me."

"Think nothing of it. I'm happy to have helped. It's good that you didn't miss flights or something by booking them immediately after the wedding. You must have seen the future," he said to Fletch before smiling and turning to me. He whispered, "Now that you're married, Shannon, I do hope you'll stop spraying painting the brick buildings downtown. If I catch you after today, I won't be able to let it slide."

I went crimson. He knew!

Chapter Thirty Eight
Prince of Tricksters

Fletch

I owed Shannon a thousand apologies. I had a room booked at a hotel downtown for our wedding night, but I didn't have a car, money to pay a taxi driver, or money to tip anyone. I had no luggage and no way to get into my apartment if we went there. I had paid for the hotel room in advance, so she didn't have to pay for that, but we had to leave in a cab.

As we pulled up to the front of the hotel, she whispered, "You're going to have to tell me what happened today."

"It was the worst."

"Must have been," she said breathily before she kissed me.

She paid the cab driver and we went into the hotel. Our room was on the second to the top floor. We took the elevator up. Since we were alone, I slammed her into the wall and kissed her like I'd die if I stopped.

When we got to our floor, I whispered huskily to her. "Want me to carry you over the threshold?"

"Nope. I want you to give me the key, and give me a few minutes before you come in."

"It's a suite. Can't you just use the bathroom or the bedroom without shutting me out?"

She thought for a moment. I knew she wanted to orchestrate that moment perfectly. Whatever outfit she had planned for our wedding night was going to be phenomenal, so I needed to give her space, but did I really need to wait in the hall?

She grabbed me by my police officer collar and pulled me along to the room. At the door, she unlocked it and dragged me in behind her.

She let me go and I smiled. Maybe that was better than carrying her over the threshold.

Except, she'd stopped in the hallway inside our suite and was staring into the bedroom with a look of pure horror across her face. Without waiting to ask her what happened, I rushed to her and saw what was causing her distress.

Carver was lying on our bed. Propped up on one elbow, he smiled at the two of us, before elegantly raising himself off the bed and approaching us. "Shannon," he said slowly. "I want something from you. I think you know what it is. Give it to me and we'll be finished."

I wasn't sure what he was talking about.

She took a deep breath. "You are the prince of tricksters. If you'd wanted to completely spoil my wedding, you could have. The only reason I'm standing here now, married, instead of a pile of pathetic white satin is because you allowed it."

I could not believe that crap came out of her mouth. It was hard on my ears to hear it, but that was exactly what Chase told her to tell him. He said Carver wanted to be the biggest man in the city. Shannon had called him the prince of tricksters. Doubtless, she'd been working on that title in order to satisfy him more completely. If he got what he wanted, they'd be finished, so I let her say what she had to without comment.

"May I say what I thought of your wedding?" he asked, with a cruel smirk in the corner of his mouth.

"I know what you thought of it. It wasn't your wedding with black decorations and gems like drops of blood hanging from the rafters."

"Your family is very homey," he continued. "I'm satisfied. Or… as satisfied as a bumpkin like you could make me. Here's your wedding gift." He pulled my wallet, keys, and phone from his pockets and dropped them on the floor.

I did not bend to pick them up.

He had one more thing to say before he left. "When I first saw you, Shannon, I thought I saw the mirror image of who I was inside, but was afraid to show. When you told your guests what it was about Fletch that got you, I saw the truth. If he and I had been switched, you and I wouldn't have had the night of my dreams. Nothing would have happened. I would have just been angry with you for not being who I wanted after you started out in such a tantalizing way. It's best that things end now." He put his hands in his pockets and strolled out.

Shannon and I stared at the spot he had occupied for a full minute before she turned to me and said, "Do you want to see if the hotel has a different room we could use?"

"Yup," I chirped without hesitation.

Chapter Thirty Nine
The Honey Part of the Moon

Shannon

When I was a little girl and dreamed about romance, I thought about where my lover would put his hands. I imagined one hand holding my neck while his other hand was at the small of my back. I imagined being eased onto the bed that way. His knees would gently part mine as he bent over me and kissed me.

I didn't give a thought as to where I'd put my hands or what I would do. I just assumed he'd know everything, like a man leading a woman on the dance floor. He'd know where we should go and how we should move.

When Fletch and I were finally alone in a new room, I had been about to dive into the bathroom to get myself ready, when I suddenly realized I was wrong. I'd never get out of another wedding dress as long as I lived, despite his reassurance that there would be many dresses and many nights where we undid each other in the dark... This was my wedding night.

I heard him lock the door behind us.

"Aren't you going to go change?" he asked, his voice husky as he waited.

"No. I thought you could help me undo my zipper."

His lips and breath were on the back of my neck and I felt his fingers on the zipper.

And suddenly, I was that girl again, who didn't know that sex could be terrible and cruel. Instead, I could be handled carefully. Fletch was going to handle me carefully. I could relax and the heat of his mouth and hands on the hard knots in my neck helped ease me to a place in my mind where I could let go of everything.

The satin fell and I let go of something indelible that I had been holding onto so tightly.

Chapter Forty
Settling Down

Shannon

Niagara Falls was little more than a hotel room in my memory, but I liked being there because no one was going to walk in on me, demand something from me, or want to see me. I could have stayed there with Fletch forever.

I also liked getting on the plane with him and going back to his apartment, that would be my apartment, and our apartment.

I went down and made friends with Evelyn who ran the fragrance shop. When she heard I'd quit working at the recording studio, she offered me a job, which I accepted. I hadn't decided exactly which design program I wanted to take, and I could certainly work at her delicious smelling shop until I figured out what I wanted.

I got my stuff from my apartment and was surprised at how little room it took up in Fletch's place. Pieces that took up a whole wall in my jewelry box apartment were little more than accents.

"I'm throwing out all your dishes," I informed him.

"I got you some boxes to do just that. They're in the corner. I'll drop them off at the thrift store on my way to work tomorrow if you've filled them up by then."

"You're cool with it?" I asked doubtfully.

"Of course, I'm cool with it. I told you I would be when you had me over for dinner. Change anything you like, but if you get an opaque shower curtain, we'll have words."

I laughed. "But there's no privacy in that bathroom. We can't have anyone visit. Can't we put up some room dividers around the toilet?"

He rolled his eyes. "It's a slippery slope. Why do you think I want to live in an apartment with the toilet out in the open?"

"So no one ever comes over?"

"Yup."

"What if I want a little privacy?"

He sighed. "Fine. Do what you've got to do around the toilet, but I meant what I said about the shower curtain."

He said that, but if I said I needed an opaque shower curtain, he would give it to me. I was fast learning, he'd give me anything.

And I loved him. I loved him much more than I ever dreamed I would.

He brought me into the part of his apartment where he made his wooden xylophones and showed me how he made them and introduced me to a Dremel tool, which I enjoyed immediately. I had wanted to leave my mark somewhere, and carving designs into the sides of his xylophones was a delight. He burned F & S Litman onto the sides of each of them before they were sold and shipped.

I left my mark everywhere.

THE END

Dear Ink Drinkers,

Congratulations on finishing this book! Thank you for reading it. I hope you enjoyed it.

Now it's confession time. There's no acknowledgments section at the end of my book because I did everything myself. I'm an independent novelist and that means that I don't have a lot of support for my little writing career. It's not a big deal or anything, but if you could leave me a review on the website you bought this book from, it would help me a lot. You don't have to say anything much, just what you thought. Books that get over fifty reviews get more notice than books that don't, so it would really help me out.

If you're too shy to write a review, that's cool. Get another one of my books and read it. That helps too.

Thank you from the bottom of my inky heart,
Stephanie Van Orman
Novelist

www.ingramcontent.com/pod-product-compliance
Lightning Source LLC
Chambersburg PA
CBHW051507030726
47592CB00006B/2148